YIPEE'S
GOLD MOUNTAIN

RAQUEL RIVERA

Red Deer Press

Published in Canada by Red Deer Press
195 Allstate Parkway, Markham, ON L3R 4T8

Published in the United States by Red Deer Press
311 Washington Street, Brighton, MA 02135

10 9 8 7 6 5 4 3 2 1

Red Deer Press acknowledges with thanks the Canada Council for the Arts and the Ontario Arts Council for their support of our publishing program. We acknowledge the financial support of the Government of Canada through the Canada Book Fund (CBF) for our publishing activities.

ONTARIO ARTS COUNCIL
CONSEIL DES ARTS DE L'ONTARIO
an Ontario government agency
un organisme du gouvernement de l'Ontario

Canada Council   Conseil des arts
for the Arts   du Canada

Library and Archives Canada Cataloguing in Publication
Rivera, Raquel, 1966-, author

Yipee's gold mountain / Raquel Rivera.
ISBN 978-0-88995-550-9 (softcover)
I. Title.

PS8635.I9435Y57 2017   jC813'.6   C2017-904205-X

Publisher Cataloging-in-Publication Data (U.S.)

Names: Rivera, Raquel, 1966-, author.
Title: Yipee's Gold Mountain / Raquel Rivera.
Description: Markham, Ontario : Red Deer Press, 2017. | Summary: "Wild West adventure of friendship, inter-cultural diversity, gender, and coming-of-age issues set in the American frontier, 1800s, between a young Chinese railway worker and Apache warrior-apprentice. Fast-paced action will appeal to a wide audience, including reluctant readers" – Provided by publisher.
Identifiers: ISBN 978-0-88995-550-9 (paperback)
Subjects: LCSH: Western stories. | Apache Indians – Juvenile fiction. | Chinese Americans – Juvenile fiction. | BISAC: YOUNG ADULT FICTION / Diversity & Multicultural.
Classification: LCC PZ7.1R58Yi | DDC 813.6 – dc23

Edited for the Press by Peter Carver
Interior and cover design by Tanya Montini
Cover images courtesy iStock

Printed in Canada

*For my parents,
Margo and Rafael,
with love*

"The mountain says, 'You should've stayed
at home.'
The mountain says, 'The world is the same,
everywhere.'"
— RAFAEL BARRETO-RIVERA, *VOICES NOISES*

"Most of them seemed intent on proving that they were right.
From their point of view, therefore,
everyone else had to be wrong."
– MARGO RIVERA, *MORE ALIKE THAN DIFFERENT*

WILD COUNTRY

The bacon popped in the pan, making sparks rise from the fire. I picked it out and dropped it into my rice pot. The rice was saved from yesterday; I was making my supplies last.

Blackie the horse shuffled among the grasses. I'd staked her on a long lead. She was a quiet one; she wouldn't go far—unless there were thieving Indians watching us.

Blackie's mane shone bright in the firelight. Her name was Blackie when I got her, even though she was all white. Maybe somebody was being funny.

I had been travelling south since leaving the Hall Ranch. Mrs. Hall had sold her herd to a big ranch and had to let me go.

"You learn quick, Yipee, and that's a fact," she told me, while pressing a five-pound bag of rice into my arms. "You're quiet, too—never did drink on Sundays, not like those other fools. I wish I could have you stay on, but it wouldn't do."

She couldn't keep a Chinese on the payroll while she was putting other men out of work—that's what she meant. There was too much trouble in that.

Mrs. Hall had taken me on to muck out her stables, just for my keep. I was given plenty of food and a bedroll in the hayloft. I'd never been near so many horses at once—all those grinding mouths and heavy, sharp feet.

But I learned that horses aren't so different from people: some are sweet and some are mean. Mrs. Hall let me ride them after a while. "Break your neck if you must," she'd said, "but don't harm the horseflesh."

On horseback I was fast, clever, and strong; we'd pull up, turn, gallop flat out—all at my command. I never wanted to get back down.

Mrs. Hall began paying me real wages that fall roundup, when we were bringing the herd all the way to market. "I suppose Yipee can ride rear," she'd told the trail boss.

Later, when she had to let me go, Mrs. Hall gave me my pay, less the cost of the supplies I'd need for my travels: kettle, pan, knife, water carrier, and blankets wrapped in a tarp for my bedroll. They were old things that she didn't need lying around, she'd said. Then she gave me Blackie.

"She's barren and oughtta be slaughtered for meat, but I can't seem to do it," Mrs. Hall said. "She's smart enough. Blackie'll get you where you're going. Any ranch that signs you on, you'll ride their stock. Cowhands coddle their own horses."

Mrs. Hall turned away but she was still talking, so I followed.

"Every cowhand needs one of these." She sneezed, brushing away the cobwebs in the back of her old shed. "It's old, but it'll get you started on your next job—'til you can buy a better one."

Mrs. Hall held out a saddle—a real working saddle. There was the horn, to hold a roped longhorn; there was the hook to hang my rope. That's where my quirt would fit, the one I had just braided. Now I could travel like I was a real cowhand.

Mrs. Hall wished me luck before I left. "It takes some pluck, little person like yourself. I half wish I could convince you to head up north. I hear they got lots of your kind on the new railroad." She gave Blackie a slap on the rump and we set off.

I would have stayed with her if I could.

The kettle was steaming; it was bath time. I picked it up, along with a pail full of creek water, and moved away from camp. I didn't want to make puddles near my bedroll.

But what was that sound?

I stopped.

"Aaooorrr!" It was a wolf howl!

Was it real? Maybe it was Indians. That's what they'd said at Mrs. Hall's—that Indians hid their signals in animal sounds. Were they out there watching me?

"That's wild country," Mrs. Hall had warned. "Those Apaches come across you, they'll steal your mount and saddle from under you—if you're lucky. If they're feeling mean, they'll hang you upside down from a tree, light a fire under you, and wait for your head to bust open."

Yes, I knew this; I'd heard the stories. The other hands liked to talk in the evenings. They'd told stories of tortures even longer, and worse, but maybe ladies didn't talk about such things.

There was an expression I'd heard the hands say, about a frying pan and a fire: I had popped out of the white man's frying pan and now I was in the Indian fire. We had an expression like that in Chinese, too, except with a tiger's mouth and a crocodile's mouth.

But there was a good chance I could find work in the New Territory of Arizona—real cowhand work. One of the older hands talked about new ranches setting up around Prescott. Lots of work there, he said. Maybe there was such a need—someone might even hire a Chinese cowhand. Mrs. Hall had hired me, after all.

I poured hot water into the pail and undressed. Starting with my face and working my way down, I scrubbed myself with a sliver of yellow soap—today was a soap day. I was shivering already. *Ai-yo*—how hellish cold the air became when I bathed—I hated it! Before, at the railroad camp, Crooked Mah always recommended to first splash cold water on the chest. This got the blood moving, he said, but it made me gasp and I could never stand it.

Jumping and puffing, I beat my dusty clothes against a tree and put them back on. By the fire, I combed out my hair and re-braided my queue. The hair above my forehead was growing in. When I got to Prescott, I would see a barber about shaving that.

As I was trying to sleep, I thought of Crooked Mah again, about when we were laying the railroad through the mountains. It had been winter; so much snow had fallen that we had to dig and dig just to reach the rock we were supposed to be digging. We made tunnels in the snow, working and living like we were moles.

The crew was laughing at me because I hid myself when I bathed.

"Ah-Yee knows modesty; he wasn't sired by no-name turtles like you all!" Crooked Mah scolded while holding up a square of tent canvas to shield me.

Then the men cooking that night's meal gave everyone a steaming bowl of rice, with a twist of salt pork and dried cuttlefish. The bad winter had kept our food order in Sacramento and there was no fresh food for the Chinese crews. The foreigners didn't seem to care for fresh food at any time. During those weeks, my mouth watered for the tang of ginger, the crunch of bamboo shoots.

Crooked Mah squatted over the rails we had laid that day, and shoveled rice into his mouth with his chopsticks. I copied him.

Shouts over a game of dice were softened by the snow walls—

the others were gambling, as usual. All the men had families back in China, waiting for this money. But the men gambled anyway—except for Crooked Mah and me.

Then I must have fallen asleep because, next thing I knew, it was as if I was really back in the tunnel, talking to Crooked Mah.

"Don't you like to gamble?" I asked him. In real life, I had never dared to question Crooked Mah, but now he answered me.

"I am a lucky man: I spend my days striking at a stone mountain with a pick and hammer." Crooked Mah's face had a problem that made it droop on one side, so I never knew when he was joking or not.

"Sometimes Boss gives me nitro to blast the mountain instead." He raised his chopsticks into the air and waved them around, "Both hands, see? Both legs. I have not blasted myself to the four winds—I am truly lucky! I save my luck for when I need it."

Then the dream went bad. There was Cooked Mah, laughing at his luck and, suddenly, his face froze, white with frost. His mouth gaped, blackened lips stretched tight across his teeth, and his eyes were cloudy—just like when we finally dug him out. When we dug the rails out.

It was an avalanche, crushing down on the tunnels. Snow rolled down the mountain, sweeping over the crew working at the front of the line. He was still standing when we got to him. His pick was still raised. His face was frozen—into a scream that had been given no air.

Next thing, I was staring at the stars. My shirt was sweaty and cold against my skin.

I got up and leaned against Blackie for a while. I stretched my arms, clutching her bulky shoulder. She was warm. She nickered in her sleep.

I had learned many more English words at Mrs. Hall's: nicker, whinny, neigh. Bit, bridle, brand. Steer. Stampede.

On the rails, Crooked Mah had made me take English lessons from the foreman—I had to pay from my own wages.

"You have no family waiting for money," Mah insisted. "This is your best chance. You must learn English."

To the foreman he said, "This one special Chinee—extra smart. He do good job for you, even pay to learn more."

The foreman took six whole dollars from my pay every month. Most Saturday nights, he gave me a lesson in his shack. He would drink a bottle of whiskey and I would practice the sounds of his harsh language. I watched the whiskey: when it got low, my teacher might smash the bottle and start screaming at some woman named "Maddy," even though we were quite alone. Other nights, his chin would just drop down to his chest and he would snore. I always left with my head full of things to practice until next lesson.

He could read and write, this teacher, and he taught me these things, too. This impressed everyone in the crew, including Crooked Mah. They all paid letter-writers to send news back home. Of course, we had no writing; we spoke our village languages.

I was warmer now. I left Blackie and stirred up the fire, putting on some new sticks. I unfolded my bedroll to air out.

That teacher was the reason I stayed on the rails after Crooked Mah died. I stayed on through that terrible winter as we blasted through the rock. At the end, I was reading Teacher's newspaper to him on Saturday nights, while the whiskey was still high in the bottle. I would have stayed all the way, until they drove the last spike into the ground—I would have stayed if I could.

RAQUEL RIVERA

CAMP

Mother was already awake. Through sleepy eyes, Na-tio could see her outside, weaving the last split branches around the staves of her basket frame. Pine gum was softening over her fire. Its sharp smell, coming through the doorway of the dwelling, must have woken him. He tied his breechcloth and stepped out, blinking.

"Where's Father?"

Mother poured the melted gum into the basket, using a scrap of fur-skin to smooth it up the sides. Once dried, it would make a fine water pot. "He's taming the new horses."

She looked up.

"My son, how can it be that you've become so tall?" Na-tio shrugged, staring at his hands as if they held the answer.

Mother offered him ground acorns and deer meat. But Na-tio wasn't hungry. He drank water from her dipper.

"They must be thirsty by now, those new horses," he said,

looking in the direction of the river. Father would have taken them for a drink, to start the training.

"Go and see for yourself," Mother suggested. "Your father could use the help."

Help? Mother wanted Na-tio to learn, that was all. He scratched and yawned, feeling lazy—he didn't want to learn today. Today he wanted only fun.

Just then, the chief's son and the rest of the boys rushed by.

"We're playing the arrow game!"

His wish was answered! Na-tio swept up his bow and quiver, hanging them across his back, while Mother protested he should eat first. In a few strides, he had overtaken all the players and was leading the way. The arrow game was something fun. Na-tio was very good at the arrow game.

The boys reached the ledge and Na-tio climbed on top.

"We'll shoot here," he announced. He was the eldest; the boys were accustomed to following Na-tio.

"I'll go first," he offered, climbing back down. Na-tio chose an old arrow from his quiver, one that did not fly quite straight because he'd set the feathers wrong. He fit it to his bow and shot into the hard-packed earth of the ledge. Now they had a target.

Na-tio's cousin was young but his aim was good. He wanted to go next—he wanted Na-tio's arrow for his own quiver. He fit his best arrow to his bow and let fly.

RAQUEL RIVERA

"*Knife and awl!*" he swore. The other boys laughed; the little one had a temper! His arrow had struck near the first, but it did not touch nor cross it.

"You wasted a good arrow to chase after a bad one," the chief's son declared. "Now watch me take yours!"

The bigger boy shot—and missed.

"Ha ha ha!"

Nobody laughed harder than Na-tio's little cousin. As another boy notched his arrow, the chief's son turned to Na-tio. "I didn't really try. I felt bad for him."

Na-tio wasn't so sure; the chief's son was not often tender-hearted like that.

Shoosh! The arrow flew and sank. It crossed Na-tio's first arrow. The marksman stepped back and looked around, that they all might see the results of this excellent shot.

Na-tio's cousin fit another arrow, eager to claim back his first.

"It's not your turn," Na-tio drew back his own bow. The little boy's arrow had a good point, hardened by fire. Na-tio wanted that arrow to study it close. He aimed and released—*shoop!*

"Ha, it touches!" Na-tio cried out before he could stop himself.

"It does not!" His cousin grew red and ran toward the ledge. It hadn't even been Na-tio's turn, either!

"It does, it does!" the others cried. "You've lost an arrow!"

The little one kicked the dirt and turned in circles, but he didn't dare pull his arrow from the ledge.

"Get away!" the bigger boys called. "We are shooting here!" Na-tio's cousin ran off, just missed by an incoming arrow.

But soon he came running back to laugh at them all. "You are too busy with your games, while the babies are using their toy arrows for something good."

The chief's son wrestled Na-tio's cousin into a headlock for being disrespectful. But Na-tio wondered what his cousin knew.

"Let him go. We will hear his news."

For a moment Na-tio's cousin looked sulky, as if he wasn't going to tell. Then he told, because the news was delicious for them all: "Honey!" he breathed, smiling at Na-tio. "They found a big hive—just further on!"

Everyone ran. This time Na-tio's cousin led the way.

The hive was a short way up the cliff, almost hidden by pines. The babies, as everyone called them, were brother and sister, visiting relatives of the chief's son. Of course, both children were long out of their cradle boards—not babies at all—but they were still very young.

That didn't stop them from shooting down chunks of the hive. When the boys arrived, the babies were carrying sticky pieces, proudly braving the angry bees' stings. Several adults had gathered to cheer them on. Mother was here, with a bag for squeezing the honeycomb. The widow was here, too, and her daughter.

Na-tio slowed to a dignified pace. The other boys flowed around him, their arrows flying high. More honeycomb fell.

Na-tio pretended to examine the stings on the babies' outstretched arms. Really, he was watching the widow's daughter prepare a smoking torch to make the bees sleepy. Her hands moved quick and sure as she wrapped grasses around a green branch. A lock of hair had escaped her maiden-tie. She kept pushing it off her face, too busy to tuck it away properly.

A good woman is a busy woman. Everyone said that. They didn't say anything about nice-looking. The widow's daughter was very pretty.

"If you want, I can talk to her." Na-tio jumped; it was the chief's son, whispering in his ear.

"What—who?" Na-tio received honeycomb from the babies. Sweet exploded in his mouth, leaving him with chewy wax between his teeth.

The chief's son only smiled, because they both knew who.

The widow's daughter and the chief's son were cousins who needn't be shy with each other. The chief's son could help her carry heavy mescal plants at harvest time, for example. The widow's daughter might ask him and Na-tio to help her and her friends, for example.

Especially if the chief's son put in a word for Na-tio.

"Yes, all right." It slipped out before Na-tio knew it. His friend's smile grew. Na-tio's face felt hot. Maybe because of the heat from the torch, now that the widow's daughter was passing near.

She greeted the chief's son; her clear, high voice rippled through the air. She gave them both a sharp glance as she hurried by. "Why do you not test your strength against the bees, instead of basking like lizards?"

Then she was gone, hidden in smoke.

When Na-tio's ears started working again, the chief's son was saying, "I'll talk to her. She's a joker, that one."

Test himself against bee stings? Bears, maybe. If there was a bear defending that hive, then Na-tio would do something. Bee stings and honey were for children. Na-tio marched off into the willows, ignoring the calls of his friend.

The low buzz of insects was good company. Leafy branches stroked his arms as he wandered alone. Na-tio didn't want fun, after all.

But he couldn't enjoy being lazy, either. It felt as if he was twitching inside his own skin. He kept walking under the bright sky.

It was good to be alone. Sometimes a person needed to think.

After a while, he heard Father's voice. Na-tio's feet had taken him to the river. Then all the different thoughts in his mind came together—as if he had known what he wanted all along.

But he needed permission. Na-tio took a deep breath and stepped out of the bush onto the riverbank.

The new horses stood, the river almost at their chests. Father, Uncle, and the chief were smoking in the shade. They were all dripping wet.

On their urging, Na-tio waded out into the water—oh, it was cold! He hoisted himself onto the nearest horse. It was tall and dark with watchful eyes.

These horses had been kept thirsty overnight. Once the warriors allowed them to drink, they had filled their bellies too full, which made them slow. Training them in the deep water kept them from getting hurt.

Na-tio's heels urged the animal against the river's gentle flow. This was a good horse. Under Na-tio's hands, tangled among the coarse hairs of the mane, the withers surged with strength and listening. Together they turned back toward the group on the shore.

Father gestured that Na-tio should bring the horse to land. As Na-tio tied the lead to a branch, the chief said, "Keep him, if you want."

Na-tio hadn't even asked!

He nodded his thanks, peeking at Father, whose face seemed to soften. Maybe it was a trick of the shadows, but Father looked a bit friendly.

Now was the moment to talk to him. Na-tio had something important to say. The chief had just given him this fine horse, after all. Na-tio was almost grown. There was only one thing left.

"Come near, Son. Your uncle was just reminding us of his first raid." Father dropped his tobacco, pushing soil to cover it.

"Yes, stay and listen," the chief added. "Your uncle tells a good story on himself!"

Na-tio approached his elders, keeping his back as straight and tall as he could.

"Uhm ... it is on that subject I would like to speak, Father." Na-tio kept his tone formal.

Father wiped his mouth. Here, under the tree, the hard planes of his face had come back. He didn't look friendly anymore.

"Speak, then. Say what you want, Son."

"Yes ... ah ... Father," Na-tio brushed a ticklish drop of water from his face. "I am grown now and I tire of hunting birds and rabbits. I wish to become a warrior."

Father looked away; his mouth made a thin line. He said nothing.

But this was Na-tio's right to ask; he had listened to the stories. He had practiced his shooting and fighting skills. He had run up and down rocky slopes to build his legs and his breath. He didn't want to play with children anymore. He didn't want the widow's daughter to boss him anymore.

RAQUEL RIVERA

Finally, Uncle spoke. "If you wish to join us on raids, that is good. As a warrior, you can win yourself honor, horses, cattle, and the other things we need. You can protect your family against neighbors who would war."

That is what Na-tio wanted.

"But you must learn first." Uncle continued. "Four raids you will ride with the warriors. You will do the work of a slave, while always speaking the noble language of the warpath. You will watch and learn the ways of the scout and the warrior. To ride with us, you must be fearless and keep a good disposition. You will not even sleep, unless you are told that you may."

Na-tio held himself still. This was what he wanted. He was sure he was ready.

Father nodded, his gaze steady on the river. The harsh cry of a raven traveled across the water. Everything else had grown quiet.

The chief addressed Na-tio. "It is settled, then. You shall begin learning with the next raid. Be modest, brave, and hardworking, and you will be invited to raid with us thereafter as a fully-grown warrior."

Na-tio understood. He had four raids in which to learn and prove his abilities. To fail was unthinkable—if he were not invited to raid after these, he'd have no means to provide for himself. He would stay poor and be ridiculed. He would never get a wife. He'd become a loner, an outcast. However difficult the challenge, Na-tio would not fail.

But he had not counted on the wait—had it always been this long between raids? He wanted to be gone!

The di-yin, Na-tio's guide during this time of learning, had loaned him the equipment he needed; he was wearing the novice cap now. Warriors fixed eagle feathers to their caps. Na-tio's cap had hummingbird pinfeathers for speed, and quail feathers because Quail bursts out of bushes, sudden and surprising, which was good for scaring enemies. He had also been given a drinking reed and a scratching stick. On the raids, he must always drink through the reed, and if he scratched himself using his hands, his skin would grow soft.

"Get away," Mother shooed at him. Na-tio was always underfoot now; he didn't enjoy playing the children's games anymore.

He found himself wandering paths the widow's daughter might use for walking to her patch of garden or to tend the horses. Na-tio had not seen her since the honey gathering. She must have heard by now that Na-tio would be going on the next raid. Maybe she would look on him differently now, with her glinting eyes. He pushed his novice cap back from his forehead.

Oh—someone was coming! It must be her!

Quick, there was no time—Na-tio vaulted behind a big rock.

Her moccasins sounded, *swish-crunch*, on the stones. She was probably carrying a pot to water her plants; or maybe she was holding a tray basket on her hip, the way she did. Na-tio pressed his lips together and forced his breathing to slow.

As the footsteps passed, he peeked out. Yes, it was her! Should he offer to carry her basket? That was silly—it was empty now. If he offered to help her gather, she would laugh at him for preferring the work of women. He pushed his novice cap forward and stepped out, watching her—*swish-crunch*—walk away.

Maybe it would be better to speak with her another day.

But another day the warriors rode out on a raid.

All the camp gathered to place pollen on Na-tio's face and sing "We all feel good and laugh," so that nothing bad would happen to him. Mother sang so loud that she lost the tune. Her mouth was twisting in a strange way.

The sun beat down on the men as they rode away from camp single file. Who knew when they would return? When they had something to bring their families. Na-tio kept his gaze fixed on the dark coat of his new, favorite horse, to rest his eyes from the glare. Each warrior carried dried meat and mescal in his pack, in case he got separated from the group. All except for Na-tio, who was allowed to carry only arrows.

Na-tio rode in the front of the line, but even he knew it was just for show. If anything happened to him on this raid, it would look very bad on the real leader. The warriors would keep the novice safe from harm.

THE CABIN

Something was wrong. There was no stock in the yard, no chickens scratching the ground. No sound came from the cabin.

It was a real built house, not a dugout in a hill with a plank for a door. There was even a window, with a glass pane and pretty curtains. If the homesteaders had moved on, they would have taken the window and the curtains with them.

I considered riding around; nobody likes a stranger. Surely the people who lived here kept guns for hunting and protection. They might mistake me for an Indian with my long, dark braid.

But my supplies were low, so I tied Blackie to a post outside the shed, on the other side of the yard. Seed was scattered on the ground, as if a bag had been spilled. Blackie leaned her head down to eat. I moved toward the silent cabin, looking for a creek or a well. I was thirsty and so was the horse.

"Good day!" I called out as I crossed the yard. That seemed

like a friendly greeting. "Good day!" I took a few more steps and called through the cabin door, "I don't want to trouble. I travel to Prescott ... there is work there." That made me sound all right. I couldn't be a thieving Indian if I had business in Prescott.

But there was only silence. The place must be deserted after all.

Wait—it sounded as if someone was moving in there.

No, no sound. I must have been mistaken.

Where had they all gone? I pushed on the door but it was blocked.

I leaned with my shoulder and pushed again and again. I saw something through the crack—was it a body?

Was that a body blocking the door?

But my shoulder had already given a great push—opening the door at the same moment as I heard a growl.

I fell through the doorway. My insides shouted: *No! Don't go that way!*

Then something flew at me—tore at me!

"*Eee!*" I screamed as I fell down on a corpse.

Then something was on top of me! "Get off, get off!" I yelled and punched into the air. Growling, snarling—rank, oily fur! Hard, heavy paws scrabbled all over me.

"*Oof—ah!*" I cried as I slid across the body onto the floor—it was so wet and sticky!

The beast jumped off me and slipped out the door into

the sunlight. Its thin, dark shape bounded into the bushes. Was that a wolf?

It must have been eating this person and got stuck in here.

I was shaking too hard to stand. The body lay between me and the door.

I had known something was wrong with this place—I should have ridden away.

I gagged on the smell of rotten meat and old gut—and what's inside guts. I spat to get the smell off my tongue. I should have smelled this from the door.

And the buzzing flies—loud as locusts—I should have heard them from the yard!

I had to get up. It was dark in here but I could see better now.

There was a woman, too, over by the window. She lay under colored lights, cast by the sunlight through her curtains. The flies were swarming in her wounds.

I choked and heaved. I saw an overturned pail with a little water left. I drank it—I had to calm down. After all this trouble, I had to find something that would be useful for me.

That's when I saw the pot in the fireplace. I scuttled over. It held porridge—hard and gluey. It would make a good, heavy lump in the belly. Blackie and I could eat this.

As I turned to leave, I noticed the baby.

He was perfect.

He still looked like a person—not like his parents. He had kicked off a small quilt. His baby-shirt had slipped up over his belly. Tight red curls were beginning to cover his round head.

But there was an arrow stuck right through him, pinning him to his cot. I dropped the porridge pot and it rolled.

We never buried Crooked Mah or the others who died in that avalanche. The ground was too frozen. But we should have; we should have buried them until their flesh fell away, leaving only bones.

I tugged the arrow from the baby. It slipped out—there was no barb to catch it. It was cut to a straight, hard spike. The wound seeped blood. I wrapped him tight in his quilt.

For Crooked Mah and the others, we should have gone back to dig up their bare bones. We should have sent them back to their home villages, to the families who waited. That's what was supposed to happen.

I held the baby close and stepped out into the sun.

There were no tools in the shed, but I used my knife and a flat rock to dig a small hole and lay the little bundle in it. The parents had been settlers; for them, home was somewhere else—their bones came from somewhere else. But for the baby, maybe this was home after all.

I wanted flowers or grass to soften the baby's grave. I looked all over the yard. Everything was so dry on this land, I returned empty-handed. There was no more waiting—I had to fill the hole. If I left the baby like this, animals would eat him.

That's when I saw more blood. As I was dropping the first handful of dirt, I saw blood on the quilt. It was soaking right through.

The dead don't bleed.

"*Ai-yo!*" I cried, pulling the little body from the ground. The dead don't bleed!

It couldn't be—he was so pale and still! My fingers were foolish and floppy as I unwrapped the quilt. It was bad that the baby was dead, but this was worse.

Because how could I keep him alive?

It was true: more blood was coming from the deep hole. Small drips they were—drip, drip, drip. Like the beat of a slowing heart.

THE PEDLAR

There was a high, small noise—*eee*. But the baby wasn't awake; I must be making this sound. He was limp and soft as I turned him over. There was no wound on his back. The arrow had not gone through as I thought. I must plug the hole. It was his only hope.

With my knife, I managed to cut the quilt without cutting my own stupid fingers. "It's all right, it's all right," I kept humming, over and over, to both of us.

"Ahhhh, that will be better," I said to the baby, as I pushed the quilt-piece into the wound. I wanted to believe this. But the quilt-piece made the baby jump in his sleep, and I almost dropped him.

He needed food. He needed his mother.

Blackie stood quietly for me while I searched through my bundles. My humming-words changed: "What to do? What to do?"

I made a sling from my empty rice sack. I wrapped another piece from the torn quilt around the baby's chest. The leftover part must keep him warm—it was so hot out here and he was still cold. I tucked him into the sling and tied it around me. Maybe my own sweaty heat would warm him. I had to go back into the cabin. There must be something there to help, something I had not seen before. There must be.

Then I heard a noise. It was a clang-clang noise—far away, but coming closer. Someone else was near!

I climbed on Blackie and gave her my heels. We galloped toward the noise, and I worried for bumping the baby too much. The clang-clang was louder and louder. We were saved! Someone else would know what to do.

This someone must be very strong to make so much noise without fear. This clatter and clang must mean they had many things—surely they had something to help the baby.

It was a covered cart, pulled by a mule-team. Pots were tied to a pole so they bumped against each other like bells. This must be a pedlar's wagon. I had seen one before, passing by Mrs. Hall's ranch. Pedlars made noise so people knew to come and buy.

The cart stopped as we came near. A very fat man leaned out from the cover's shadow. "What d'you need?"

Before I could tell him, he called over his shoulder. "S'all right, Ben. It's safe to come out." The pedlar wore a broad hat tied under his chin. I could hardly see his face, but his eyes were sharp and turned on me.

RAQUEL RIVERA

"A little Injun like you–" he told me, "–you wouldn't cause trouble now, would'ya." It didn't sound like a question. The pedlar pulled back his coat so I could see the rifle on the seat next to him.

"No problem for me!" I called. I waved and hoped that seemed friendly.

A small child climbed from the back, eyes big. "There is a hurt baby here." I pointed to my sling. "I look for help before he dies."

The pedlar rubbed his face, muttering, "Three days' travel and still no sale." He sighed. "Bring it here." He jerked his head. "Let's have a gander."

I urged Blackie to the cart and pulled the sling off my neck. "It's a he," I told the peddlar, "same as Ben." The child jumped to hear his name in my mouth. I was sorry for this; I didn't want to scare him. He was so young, almost a baby, too. But I thought the pedlar wasn't right to call the baby "it." He needed to know.

The pedlar peeked into the sling. "This child is white!"

His sharp eyes turned to slits. His mouth went hard. "What're you doing with a white woman's baby?"

"I found him in the cabin. His parents are dead." It was all I wanted to say about that.

The pedlar stared some more, then nodded. "He's unconscious– hardly breathing." His hands were careful as he pulled the different pieces of quilt. His voice went soft as he turned to Ben. "You know the bottle I drink after supper? Go on and fetch it for me."

Ben's short legs dangled before he dropped from the driver's bench and disappeared into the cart.

As the pedlar poured drops from the bottle onto the baby's chest, I thanked the luck that crossed our path. If anyone could keep him alive, it was this fat pedlar. Look at how well Ben listened and fetched, even though he was only small. Look at how the pedlar re-tied the wound with a clean bandage.

I was breathing again, slow and steady. Blackie felt warm and comfortable under me. If it was just the two of us again, we could manage anything.

I wondered why the pedlar was unwrapping his coat. Maybe he would keep the baby closer this way. Now he was unbuttoning his shirt, which was very strange. Oh!

I gasped. The pedlar was holding the baby to his breast—he was a lady!

Blackie huffed and backed up—I must have tugged on her bit.

Ben was surprised, too. He cried and pulled on the pedlar's coat. But the pedlar put the baby on that big stomach and put his— her—breast to the baby's mouth. "Mine!" Ben shouted, but the pedlar kept him away.

We all watched but the baby did not drink. He did not know there was food for him. He was still asleep. The pedlar made him drink anyway. A few drops on his lips, then into his mouth.

"There, there." The pedlar held the baby with one arm. With

RAQUEL RIVERA

the other, she rocked crying Ben close to her side.

I dismounted and climbed up to her cart-seat to help her tie the sling around her neck. "It's a handy contraption," she said, and I felt a little bit proud. "Dunno if the little tyke'll make it. I'll do my best. If he's still among the living by the next time I see folks, I'll get him settled if I can." I helped her wrap the big coat around them both.

"You want I come with you?" I asked. It all seemed too much for one pedlar to do.

"No, child, bless us—look at you! How'm I gonna sell my wares, explaining the likes of you?" She shooed Ben into the shade of the cart again and took the reins.

I jumped down and stood by Blackie, waving them all goodbye. I was glad I could still go to Prescott.

She leaned out to me with a little smile as the mule-team started off. "I got three more back at home with their big sister— this is a holiday for me!"

CHAPTER

5

RAID

Na-tio slid off his horse and dropped to the ground. Sweat flecked the animal's shoulders. Na-tio lay still. He'd torn the skin from his elbow when he landed but it didn't hurt. Pebbles and grit stuck to the wound but he wouldn't move. Not yet.

They weren't chasing him or they would have caught up by now. They'd let him go—all of them. They must hate him. Father must hate him.

The sun was blistering—the horse was dry already. Na-tio fumbled for his drinking reed. There was still dew pooled in the base of the aloe plants. He crawled over and sipped it down.

Father's eyes came back to him—shiny and flat they had gone, like the skin of a fish. Na-tio didn't know him anymore. And Father had just stared, like Na-tio was somebody different, too.

Na-tio forced his breathing to slow. The dew cooled his throat. He picked the stones out of his elbow and found his novice cap.

Should he put it back on?

He led the horse toward the cottonwoods in the distance. He shouldn't have ridden that hard, not with only a single horse to carry him. There might be more water near the trees.

It was only that he hadn't expected the killings.

A raid was for taking, for gathering needed supplies. Why kill when you might need to raid again another time? That was how raiding was—how it was supposed to be. Raiding was not war. He hadn't been ready, that was all.

It had been a small place: a cow, chickens. Na-tio had gone ahead to scout with Father and Uncle. They'd sneaked through the bush, right up to the cabin, under the window.

There had been only two: there was a woman inside the cabin and someone else was in the shed, making pounding noises. Uncle crept around the cabin. Father motioned that Na-tio should follow him to the shed. Na-tio noticed good iron on the ends of the diggers and planters that leaned there; iron was useful. They could tell the chief and the others what they found, then come back at night to collect what they wanted.

Now Na-tio's horse was blowing hard—he must be very thirsty. They were at the trees, but the water that fed them had gone underground in the heat. At least there was shade.

Where should Na-tio go? Could he go back to camp, to Mother? Should he return to the farm and try to track the raiders?

Would they give him another chance? Would Father's eyes have changed back to normal?

Na-tio didn't want to think about it right now.

First, he must take care of the horse. He had ridden past a good creek not too far from the farm. The horse must have a drink. He mounted and turned them both back the way they had come.

RAQUEL RIVERA

6

THE OLD STORIES

"We are a strong people, Yip Yee. You've heard us called devils and pests, although we work harder and smarter than these foreigners that abuse us. We prosper, even with nothing but dirt: we turn swamps into fields and orchards; we sift gold from the silt of the river; and there is good money in scrubbing the filthy foreigners' shirts. But when we succeed, we are robbed and beaten; we are chased from our claims, our homes, and our shops."

Crooked Mah told good stories. Even when he talked of bad things, everyone listened. When he talked of good things, their dreams flew high.

"There were placer miners, good Chinese men, who found a forty-pound nugget not far from here—thousands of dollars in gold in one magic moment!" Crooked Mah's own pan glinted with the sand that careful sifting would turn into a few dollars. This was before the railroad job, when we worked a small claim with a group of partners.

"What do you think they did? Did they run like fools to town and weigh in for their money?" I shook my head. The partners laughed as they sifted. We'd all heard the story before.

"They chiseled it down, selling small pieces among handfuls of gold dust. They hid the secret of their wealth from the foreigners, who would certainly rob them of their good fortune if they knew."

After I gave away the baby, Crooked Mah often came to me and told me his stories. But now they made my head hurt.

If only Crooked Mah would visit me with stories about this place! There was a creek near the farm that still held running water in the bottom. Blackie and I camped here. All my food was gone and the porridge pot was empty.

But there were many frogs, and it was lucky that I knew how to catch and roast them—we had often enjoyed them on the claim.

Crooked Mah used to know everything, but he had no stories for this place. Here there were crab-like creatures, with high curling tails, that scuttled among the rocks. There were trees that grew long pods, and prickly plants with fat red fruits. Which of these would feed me and which was poison?

The first thing I could ever remember was Crooked Mah scrubbing shirts over a tub. We scrubbed for laundries in San Francisco, then Sacramento. I never had a mother. I didn't know I was supposed to have one until later on. Whenever I asked, Crooked Mah said he was like my mother and my father, so I owed

RAQUEL RIVERA

him double obedience, and I was not to think about such things anymore. Anyway, there were no mothers in Chinatown. I never saw any women—except those sad creatures who lived in the cages by the dock.

We saved our money from the laundry work and bought into a mining claim in the mountains. Our group paid a low price to a white miner who thought it was used up. He wanted to rob us, but we found enough gold left behind to earn the price back twice again. "Foreigners are sloppy, Yip Yee. They are not careful, so they lose their fortune."

What would Crooked Mah do now? We had always worked; I needed work that would pay.

Blackie and I had traveled far. Surely we were near Prescott by now.

Blackie was leaner than when we started, stronger, and her coat shone. Her eyes were clear and bright. I reached up and held her long face in my hands. I stroked her soft, smooth nose.

"What will happen to us?" I whispered into her nostril, since her ear was too high.

Did I dare take us farther on? We had to move sometime. I must get to Prescott or find paying work along the way. I came from a strong people, after all.

Blackie sneezed.

7

NEW PERSON

But what kind of a person was this? Not a true person such as himself, Na-tio was almost certain. He dressed like an Anglo, a white man, in boots and cloth and a wide-brimmed hat. Was he Mexican? Na-tio had never seen a free Mexican before, only those that were brought back from the warpath. He knew that they had farms and ranches, with livestock and other useful materials. A good raid began and ended in Mexico, Father said. Mexicans were also soldiers, like Anglos but worse. Betrayers, Father called them, enslavers and child-stealers. Everyone hated Mexicans since long before the Anglos came.

Na-tio settled behind the mesquite; he mustn't be seen. He would wait until dark and take the horse and saddle. Na-tio would bring them back as a gift for Father. If Na-tio brought back a horse, well, it was almost as if he had continued to raid on his own, wasn't it? Maybe that was all right for a novice to do.

Anyway, it had been that Anglo who'd started it all, back at the cabin. That man who'd been making pounding noises in the shed. Na-tio and Father had crept in the shadow of the shed wall, by all the iron-tipped tools.

The man must have been clumsy. He must have pounded on himself because there was a shout, the sound of a tool dropped, and then all noises stopped.

The shed door slammed open and the man ran out, calling for his wife. He held one hand across his front like it was a baby; there was blood on his shirt.

In his rush, he kicked over a full bag—seed spilled across the ground. He stumbled and cursed, and his face turned back to the shed. He was looking their way, eyes squinting against the hard sun.

Na-tio stiffened, even though he knew he and Father were invisible in the shadow.

That was when it all started—when Father saw the Anglo's face.

Father twitched and went rigid. Na-tio could hear him breathing—in and out—long, hard gasps.

Father was angry. His body was shaking with it. In the shadow, Na-tio felt cold. What was making Father so angry?

Father grabbed the axe that leaned with the other tools against the shed. At the same moment, the woman rushed out of the cabin, wiping her hands on her skirt. Father sprang out, axe raised high.

But there had been no dance!

Father's face was unpainted—he was wearing his clothes—he was not ready for war!

This was supposed to be a raid!

Uncle slipped out from behind the cabin door and grabbed the woman by the hair. She cried out—sharp, shrill—but went silent when Father scraped the axe across the man's forehead. The Anglo screamed as his scalp tore away and fell into the dust. Father stomped on it and let out a war cry.

"I know this one—this is the one!" Father dragged the screaming man into the cabin as he passed Uncle. "He will die slow for what he did to us!"

Uncle had his arm across the woman's mouth and nose; her eyes were bulging like a frog's. So were Uncle's.

Na-tio followed Father, pulling an arrow from his quiver before he even knew it.

It was a silly thing to do—there was nothing to shoot. Na-tio was trembling as bad as Father but he didn't feel angry. What had this Anglo done to Father—to us? Na-tio tried to make his face still like a mask but he couldn't; he wasn't yet a warrior.

And besides, this was supposed to be a raid!

The wounded man rolled and cursed on the floor as Father hacked at his arms, his legs, and, finally, his chest and his belly. "Wife-killer, baby-murderer," Father growled between the blows.

In the doorway, the woman fought with Uncle, reaching back

for his face with claw-fingers. She rammed the heel of her boot against his shin. Uncle grunted with pain and slit her throat. Then she was quiet. He let her slide down.

"You should have kept her!" Father cursed. "To slave for the women." He was covered in the other man's blood, but it wasn't enough. His anger still boiled. His eyes had gone flat. Na-tio didn't know him. Uncle stepped away.

"It is better that she is dead. She was too much trouble." Uncle spoke low and smooth, like when he was taming a horse.

Father dropped the Anglo's body; it thumped to the floor. He pulled up the woman and threw her across the room like she was a husk doll.

"Better that she is dead," he finally agreed. "Let the whole family be dead, like he made mine."

Uncle moved to the Anglo. He prodded the body with his foot. "So this is the one who would creep up on our family and slaughter them like quail." He turned, stepping over the woman, to look out the window. "I was only a child when it happened. My sister, my nieces who played with me, all gone. For a long while after, I thought you had turned to stone."

Father's face was heavy with remembering. "I watched him pass me. I wanted no trouble; my horse was burdened with deer meat for my family. Further along, I saw what he had done—first wife, our pretty girls. How long I have regretted letting him go on his way." The axe flew across the room, sinking its head into the log wall. "He sent them to the afterlife without their scalps—now he goes without one, too."

"Now first family is avenged," Uncle agreed. Then, for some reason, he pulled the curtains shut. The sun shone through the pattern of bright colors—flowers from another land.

Those curtains had danced in Uncle's hands. But Na-tio didn't want to think about it right now. He forced his mind back to the Mexican below.

The Mexican had been catching frogs for a while now. He had skinned a good pile and was driving them in rows onto long spikes made from green branches. Why?

Na-tio's nose tickled but he did not scratch. He crept across the open ground to the low saltbush, closer in. If this Mexican was making frog-magic, Na-tio wanted to hear his song.

The Mexican built up a fire with sticks and leaves. Smoke rose.

Na-tio squatted back on his heels and finally used his scratching stick on his nose. Would a lone Mexican make a daytime fire so far from home? His smoke will be seen from all around! Maybe this was no Mexican after all.

The strange person drove the sticks of frogs into the ground, so they leaned toward the fire. He propped them with stones to keep them steady.

The smell wafted to Na-tio through the loose branches of the saltbush. Every so often, the stranger would carefully turn a stick. Na-tio waited for the song.

The stranger dipped into a pot with a sprig of broom. He painted something onto the hot frogs.

Fat; it smelled like animal fat drifting his way. Maybe by feeding the frogs, the stranger charmed out the magic.

Na-tio's belly felt empty; he hadn't eaten. He tore leaves from the saltbush and chewed. Oh, no—his foot slipped on the rocks! A small landslide of pebbles rolled down the slope toward the stranger's camp.

The stranger went very still. He turned around. *Knife and Awl*—he was looking Na-tio's way!

That white hat covered his eyes, but Na-tio knew that stranger must be looking up—right in his direction!

Now Na-tio must call on his own magic. How stupid he'd been, how loud! Na-tio faded into the land—he must be like rock. He must send away his restless spirit before it caught the stranger's eyes. He hoped the feathers on his cap would break up the outline of his dark hair—no, don't hope. Hope makes noise.

The stranger was walking up the slope, listening for the next sound and watching for movement. Did he suspect that there was a spy watching? Or was he thinking of catching a meal?

Na-tio tried to let go of the questions. He was stone; stone didn't wonder. He let his breath grow shallow, just like Uncle had taught him. He dropped his eyelids halfway, and did not care whatever he saw. Stone didn't care.

The footsteps were coming near. Stone closed the flap inside his ears. The footsteps crunched past the saltbush and the stranger came into view again, this time very close. Round smooth cheeks could be seen under the white hat; the nose, small and flat, was almost buried between them. The stranger turned this way and that. A thick braid fell straight down his narrow back.

Stone saw all this and tried to push away thoughts: that the face was soft like a girl's; the hair fell straighter and heavier than his own; the shirt was like the one Father had brought back from a raid and wore only on special occasions. These thoughts must be released before the stranger noticed them.

For a moment they were still, the stone and the stranger. The stranger's head turned, scanned the land too high, and saw nothing at his feet.

Then he walked back down to his frogs and painted them some more.

Oh, *yechh!* He was eating them!

The stranger had packed most of the dry, blackened frogs into his bag, keeping back one last stick-full. He was now tearing off the legs, one after another, and stripping the meat with his teeth!

Frogs!

RAQUEL RIVERA

If Na-tio's stomach had not been so empty, he might have vomited on the ground. He shuddered—next the stranger will be eating snake!

Na-tio had discovered a very new kind of person indeed! He slipped away, back to his own horse waiting on the other side of the slope. The stranger had prepared and packed enough food— well, frogs—for a journey. Where did he plan to travel? What was his purpose on the land? Na-tio would find out. He would not take the stranger's horse just yet.

Something had woken him. Na-tio's night eyes were coming back; he looked around.

The stranger was still, a mound under blankets. The horse's head dropped low in sleep. Na-tio pricked his ears—had it just been a bad dream?

"*Whoo-hoo, whoo-hoo!*" No—it was Owl.

This was bad, to cross paths with Owl, messenger of the dead; now someone will certainly die.

Na-tio gathered up his own blanket and tied it to his horse. He strapped on his quiver and his bow. He couldn't sleep here, not with Owl nearby. He didn't want to leave the stranger so soon, but it was necessary.

He crept toward the glowing campfire. Na-tio would just collect the stranger's horse and then leave.

But he felt a whisper of movement through the air—someone was already in the camp! He waited.

Eyes flashed in the night. Some shadow—swifter than Na-tio—was stalking the sleepers.

The shadow slipped through the dark and, before Na-tio could blink, it landed on the hindquarters of the stranger's horse. The horse woke up screaming; she danced forward, but her hobble kept her from running hard.

The stranger jumped from his blankets and rushed to his horse. He hadn't yet seen the shadow tearing at her flank.

Na-tio notched an arrow while running to get his shot—*shoop!* Na-tio's arrow struck. The shadow dropped from its prey. It was big! It was Wolf—a very bold wolf! Na-tio notched another arrow. The hunter had been silent in its attack, but now, defending meat, it warned Na-tio away.

The stranger tried to calm his shocked horse, leading her from the growling beast.

Na-tio turned his back on the glowing coals; they were making it difficult for him to see. The wolf seemed to have no such problem. It rushed Na-tio, the arrow shaft bouncing from its side like a thin, useless limb.

Na-tio aimed but his target was too narrow, too fast—moving straight at him. Wide feet smacked his chest, toppling him, crushing the breath out of him. There was a dull, deep pain in his

RAQUEL RIVERA

head as he fumbled for his knife at his thigh—he thrust up, in—farther, higher!—and across.

The wet, warm life of the animal washed over him. The terrible pressure on his head was gone.

He felt the weight of the hunter's body roll off his own.

Gentle hands touched his ragged skull.

CHAPTER

8

THE INDIAN

There was a big rip in his scalp—a flapping hole in his thick hair. His cap had helped to protect one side of his head. I felt for other wounds. The Indian was awake but he allowed this.

He'd saved us. It seemed unlikely he would torture me now.

But I had no salve, no bandages. I didn't drink, so I had no alcohol to clean the wound. I put the kettle on the fire. I would prepare the last of my tea; it might strengthen him.

As the water heated, I felt along Blackie's ripped flank. She skittered but I was gentle. Her breathing was steady. Maybe her wounds were not serious—dammit for being so dark! How could I be expected to do anything in this dark?

The Indian shifted on the ground—he was watching us. I stroked Blackie, long and smooth, along her neck, shoulders, and hard round sides. I didn't even have any sugar left to offer her. "There, there," I couldn't help murmuring.

RAQUEL RIVERA

Blackie settled; she even dropped her head to browse for a moment. I hurried to bring her some water in the pail—she drank. Maybe this was a good sign?

A cowhand does not love his horse; I knew that. Horses are tools, to be fed and watered for only as much work as you can get out of them. A cowhand's horse has a short and difficult life, ridden hard among wild, bad-tempered longhorn.

But Blackie had been good company. I would never have been able to make this trip without the distance she covered in an easy day's travel. And she was still my best chance of getting to Prescott in good health.

I clucked at her and flicked her tail. She balked; then she took a few steps forward. I'd wait until light before asking her to walk some more.

Back by the fire, I dumped the last of my tea into the kettle. I filled the tin cup and brought it over to the Indian. He was still awake, still watching. He sat up, very slow, and drank. He said something that I did not understand. Then he spoke again.

"You drink Anglo drink."

The Indian spoke English!

"Tea? Yes, but tea is not foreigner drink."

"I know tea." He held the cup out to me. "Sugar?" I shook my head and he sighed. He took the cup back and drank it down. He lay back on the ground. I gave him one of my blankets.

"You don't speak Mexican. You not Mexican?" he asked.

"Chinese." I told him and, all of a sudden, I was very tired—so tired, I couldn't keep my head straight on my neck.

"Sleep," I suggested to the Indian. But he was already snoring.

He knew many useful things, this Indian. He showed me how to scrape gum from tree bark to use on Blackie's wounds and his own. We dissolved it in water. I chased after his horse and cut a strip from the blanket in his bundle. He soaked it in the water and I bandaged his head. Then I washed Blackie's rump with the gummy water.

She was limping. I supposed I ought not to ride her for a while until she was stronger.

There was also the wolf. We skinned it.

At the mining claim, I had helped to cut up a young pig once, but I'd never skinned a furry creature. The Indian cut a line along the underside, working through the stabbing cuts he'd made the night before. He pulled back the fur and slipped his knife under the skin, separating it from the muscle and pulling some more. Each time he pulled, he'd turn to me. "All right? All right?"

I nodded and took his place with my own knife. He fell back on the ground. He didn't look very well.

I was careful not to jab through the skin. When I got to the legs, the Indian pushed himself up and showed me how to peel it

52   RAQUEL RIVERA

down and cut through the joints at the feet. By the time I'd done the first side, sweat was running into my eyes. I took my kerchief from around my neck and tied it around my forehead, stuffing my hat back on. Now we both wore bandages.

"Here." The Indian held out a thin strand that he'd pulled off a bush. He kept one for himself and broke it open—there were seeds inside—it was like a peapod! The peas were sweet and juicy. We collected more and ate.

Then I finished skinning the wolf. The Indian showed me how to roll up the wolf skin, messy side in.

The day was hot now. The Indian looked gray and shiny. We both crawled under the bushes by the creek. I fell asleep.

I woke up with a jump—I'd fallen asleep and left the Indian alone—had he taken my things? Blackie—where was Blackie?

There she was! She'd wandered under the trees with the Indian's horse.

So the Indian hadn't slipped away.

He was cutting up the wolf. I pulled the twigs out of my hair and went to help him.

We cut thin slices from the haunch and laid them on bushes to dry out. By nightfall, we had a big chunk speared over the fire. I brushed it with the fat I'd saved from my bacon—this meat had no fat of its own.

Suddenly there was nothing to do. We'd been so busy all day and now we just sat. The Indian kept staring at me.

I saw to Blackie. I re-tied her to the big tree so she would not get loose again. I slowly reached out toward the other horse's nose. Would he be mean? He didn't try to bite.

I went back to the fire. That Indian was still staring.

"You are ... Chinese." He said the word with care.

I nodded and then he nodded. It was quiet again.

"Now you speak Chinese," he suggested with a wave of his hand—it flitted like a moth in the firelight.

It had been a while since I had spoken Chinese out loud. I picked up the kettle and pointed to the leaves in the bottom

"*Chai,*" I told him, "means tea. *Fu,*" I tapped on the kettle. "*Huo,*" I said, poking among the coals. I looked around for other words I could tell him. "*Mah,*" I said, gesturing toward his horse standing next to mine. *Fan* was an important word, but I couldn't show him because my rice was all gone. What else could I say? All around me there were strange plants and trees. I had no words for these.

The Indian's eyes widened and he looked up at the tall trees that shaded us. "*T-ees,*" he called them. He gestured to a spiky-looking bush and said, "*Nadah.*" Then he touched the pot that held my bacon fat. "*Ik-ah,*" he said. Surely these were not English words. They must be the words of his people.

RAQUEL RIVERA

"My name is Yip Yee," I patted my chest.

"Na-tio," he touched his own. He picked up the cup and asked, "More chai?"

I pulled the soggy leaves from the kettle and squeezed them, shaking my head. "They are finished." The Indian nodded—Na-tio nodded.

I offered him my frogs, roasted only yesterday and still tasty. But he pushed them away, closing his eyes.

I heard Blackie huffing and stamping. Na-tio's horse was nosing her rump.

"It is good your horse is female," Na-tio said, and turned to me, squinting.

"Two males cannot stay side by side," he said, looking me up and down. "Too much fighting."

I nodded, keeping my eyes fast on the horses.

He went back to staring.

SKIN

The mare was not too hurt, so Na-tio and the Yipee person started off. It was early, when the air was still fresh and cold. Na-tio had offered to guide, since Prescott was not far. This seemed to make Yipee very happy.

What else was there for Na-tio to do? He needed time to think and let his head heal. He mustn't go back to camp, not like this, wounded and empty-handed. He would seem pitiful, a failure—that must not be so. He was still raiding—he could still succeed.

The inside of the cabin came back to him now; the dead woman's hair had come loose and brushed across the floor, as she rolled to the wall. After Father had tossed her.

Na-tio did not know him. Father's face had gone heavy, his hand resting against the wall where he had sunk the axe. After speaking of first family, he seemed too tired to stand. Father had never spoken of them before.

Uncle had replied, soft and low, that first family was now avenged. Then he'd looked out the window and pulled the curtains shut—blocking the sun from peering in. But light still shone through the bright-colored flowers on the Anglo cloth.

Then someone in the cabin had laughed.

Na-tio's feet uprooted from the floor and moved him toward the sound. It was a baby!

In the strange way of babies, it had slept though the shouts and thumps, but had woken to the pretty lights from the flower curtain. The baby was laughing at the colors.

The laughter made Father jump. He pulled the axe from the wall, full of anger again.

Uncle's eyes darted to Na-tio and the baby, then back to Father. "We can take the baby," he suggested. "Your wife will adopt it."

Father looked as if he might throw the axe at Uncle. "Were my children adopted?" he shouted. "Or were their faces smashed in with the butt of a rifle?" Na-tio's stomach came up. He didn't know this story. He didn't know anything anymore.

"We do not keep this man's child!" Father cried, axe raised. Father's anger was correct, so why did Uncle look upset? Why did Na-tio want to vomit? There was so much blood already. Father moved toward the baby but Na-tio blocked him. Na-tio didn't mean it; he just moved. He moved against Father.

Now Father's flat eyes were driving into Na-tio. There was no thinking after this; Na-tio's hand rose and fell—his arrow plunged straight down. There hadn't even been a cry.

The cabin was still.

Father stood over Na-tio as if frozen. Na-tio had never moved against Father before; that was very wrong. But now the baby was dead, as Father wanted. Na-tio couldn't stop trembling. There seemed to be no good way. He didn't want any of this. He didn't want to know what was done to first family. But it was too late now.

He didn't want to keep the murderer's baby, like Uncle said, and call him brother.

But he didn't want the baby dead, either. His hand had done it. His hand still gripped the arrow as Na-tio trembled, gasping for air.

Uncle reached out and laid a gentling hand on Father's back.

"Brother-in-law, my brother," was all he said. The axe dropped to the floor. Uncle moved to Na-tio, but Na-tio didn't know anybody anymore. He ran.

He had run away, straight for his horse—even now, Na-tio's heart thumped, remembering how it had pounded in that wild dash from the cabin.

He didn't want think about it right now. Na-tio commanded his heart to settle.

To be in the world, one must be strong and fearless. Were the hills and canyons afraid? Of course not. Father was a skilled raider and a fierce warrior—he did not kill for fun. Death was part of life. That Anglo had it coming. But did the baby deserve to die?

He tried to hold Father in his mind—Father as he really was. Long ago, when Na-tio's legs were still fat and stubby, he was waiting with the other boys for the men to return. Of course, the biggest boys had jostled for the better places in front, where it was certain they would receive the reins from the triumphant raiders. They would have the honor of leading the horses away and seeing to their care.

Na-tio wanted this, too, but he was little and had been shoved to the back. But he still hoped he might be given the reins—he might.

Now Na-tio could see how silly this dream had been: a small child—almost a toddler—leading a full-grown horse, thirsty and wild from the raiding trail.

But he had been just a child. He didn't know. The sounds of the horses were coming near. The boys were ready.

First the chief arrived. He dismounted and gave over his horse. Others did the same. The women watched, breathless, until every rider came into view.

Joyful cries and songs were unleashed—no one had been lost! They had so many good things from the raid, and no family need mourn in their dwelling tonight.

It was at times like these that Father smiled.

Standing straight on his short legs, Na-tio watched as Father rode past one big boy, then another. Na-tio stopped breathing–Father was riding past everyone. Father was riding to him!

Father's horse was especially big, as befitted Father's own tall, broad frame. Its shoulders gleamed with sweat as it snorted and tossed its great head. Na-tio did not run from the stamping hooves.

Father dismounted and, with the warmth of the sun behind his eyes, he gave the reins to Na-tio.

Then Na-tio had felt himself lifted up. He remembered seeing his own chubby legs stretched across the wide saddle. In this way, Na-tio helped Father bring his horse to the creek. That was Father.

Na-tio's head started to ache, comparing the memory of Father like this with the picture of Father in the cabin. He couldn't see them together.

And Na-tio had disobeyed Father's wishes. Sweat trickled from under his head-bandage. He wouldn't think about what else he had done.

He looked back at Yipee, under that old white hat, shifting comfortably from side to side in that cracked saddle, while the pale mare picked her way along.

Na-tio focused on the mare's shoes–iron, nailed into the hoof. His own horse wore strong hide boots, tied tight with a drawstring. The hooves themselves had been painted with many layers of liver and limestone paste to make a hard crust. Na-tio's horse wouldn't be limping on this journey.

He liked showing Yipee things: it proved that he did know something—despite what others might think. The narrow, round-cheeked stranger was quite helpless, like a child who doesn't know yet.

But Yipee also had determination and some courage, and he had a plan of some kind. Na-tio respected this.

They traveled higher and higher. The morning chill burned away, and the hot air waved before them. Spiny plants and bush gave way to bigger trees. By nightfall, they would be among the pines. The sun moved high, then low.

If he were any younger, Na-tio would be bothered by hunger now. But raiders traveled for days and nights without sleep or food whenever necessary. Still, it was a pity that it was not yet the season for pine seeds. Na-tio enjoyed roasted pine seeds very much.

He kept his eyes open for a chance to raid. They might come across a corral of horses. Did that Yipee know how to cut a horse from the group? Between them, they might take as many as three horses each. Six horses! Now that would be something to bring back from a raid! Father would smile at that.

Or maybe they would find cattle instead. Or sheep.

Like magic, on a far crest to the west, a wisp of smoke appeared in the cooling purple sky. This must be a sign! Maybe the people-who-weave-blankets were camping over there. No doubt they had a great many horses, cattle, and sheep with them. Na-tio turned his horse to the smoke. He would lead Yipee to where they could spy on the camp—it was not so far out of their way.

It was not as Na-tio had hoped.

The camp was small: one square canvas tent and only three horses corraled nearby. Several dogs ran at them, driving them from the trees, right into the camp. By the fire hunched a great furry giant.

He rose, sweeping up his rifle and aiming.

Yipee's horse reared at the dogs. He held on and settled her back down, but both horses continued to dance in protest at the snapping creatures. The giant called them off.

"Here—what've we flushed out?"

The giant spoke Anglo. He wore a wolf skin across his shoulders, making him look as wide as he was tall. His face was covered in hair, in the way of Anglos and some Mexicans.

Yipee spoke. "I travel to Prescott. I look for work on a ranch. Do you know ranches nearby?"

The giant kept the rifle trained on them. "And who's that?" He tilted his head in Na-tio's direction. Na-tio kept still. It was better not to talk too much.

Yipee answered, "He guides me."

"You're a strange pair of kids." The giant lowered his gun.

"You got food—wolf meat? Can't stand it. Never mind, you can camp here for the night if you want."

Na-tio and Yipee dismounted. The giant ordered the dogs to the fire. "Fiend, Fury, Satan—get down!"

For a moment, Na-tio wished he hadn't led them this way after all, but the giant was shaking a pouch of tobacco at him, and Na-tio rather liked tobacco.

"Nice hair." The giant reached out and tugged Yipee's long braid as they brought the horses around the tent to graze with the others. "What are you? Some kind of California Indian?"

"I'm American," Yipee said. Na-tio's eyes flickered at that and the giant noticed it.

"Yeah, I don't believe him, neither," he said.

As they passed the tent, a bad smell hit Na-tio. Many raw wolf skins were hanging from a rope pulled between two trees. Some were fresh, like Na-tio's own, but most had dried and hardened without being tanned. What could the giant want with so many skins in this disgraceful state, twirling like empty corpses? He showed no respect for the animals he hunted.

"You got yourself a wolf, too," the giant said, as Na-tio unloaded his bundle from the horse. They walked back to the fire, chewing tobacco.

"Some towns are paying as much as ten dollars a skin, if the ranchers are losing enough stock."

Yipee sat down on his bedroll. "So that is your work? You hunt wolves?"

The giant smiled but he didn't tell them the joke. "Wolves and other things. Whatever pays." He turned to Na-tio. "How'd you get yours?"

Na-tio preferred not to speak about this, but the skin-collector was waiting for an answer. Finally, Na-tio pulled out his knife to show how.

"That cut your tongue out?" the skin-collector asked. "Look, Indian, I share my tobacco and my fire with you. You can act civil or you can get out."

Na-tio did not like this man.

"Wolf jumped me. See, hurt." Na-tio pushed his cap to show the bandage on his head

"Na-tio was saving my horse," Yipee added. "Saving me."

The skin-collector smoothed his beard from his lips. "I prefer to use dogs; they get my wolf every time. Sneaky, cowardly things— that's wolves for you."

Na-tio knew that wolves were like people; they wanted to travel and hunt together, to better care for their young. The skin-collector got up and went into his tent. A moment later he came out with a bottle. He took a drink and passed it to Na-tio. Na-tio knew this drink. Some people liked this Anglo drink—it was sociable. But Na-tio didn't like the way it made his head spin, so he pretended to gulp, only wetting his lips. He passed it to Yipee, who swallowed and coughed. Yipee gave the bottle back to the skin-collector, who took a big swig and kept it.

"One time I was riding with my dogs—this was up Utah way— and this wolf jumps out of the grasses and hits the side of my mount, tearing up my leg good. First time I ever seen the front end of a wolf like that—they're mostly running away," he snorted.

"I'd stumbled on a nest of 'em. That's the only thing that'll make a wolf stand and fight. I worked my rifle out of its case and blew that bitch-wolf's head clear off. The dogs finished off the nest."

He took another gulp of his drink. "I don't let 'em do that anymore. I leave the pups to grow; their skins'll pay better when they're grown." He seemed pleased by his clever thinking. His beard was wet and messy. His eyelids kept dropping down. He thrust the bottle at Na-tio, who pretended to drink and gave it back.

"Don't forget your friend, the *American*." The skin-collector passed the bottle to Yipee.

"I am American," Yipee insisted. "California is State—part of United States. I was born in San Francisco Harbor."

The skin-collector squinted. "San Francisco; that explains it. You must be one of them Chinee." He reached for the bottle. Yipee gave it back without taking a drink.

Na-tio couldn't make sense of their talk. Yipee was no more American than he was; that was obvious.

But Yipee was talking new nonsense now. "We sell our wolf skin to you?" he asked the collector. "For only eight dollars. You make two dollars like this."

The skin-collector laughed but he didn't sound happy. "I might give you two dollars—maybe," he said.

Na-tio thought he'd rather keep the skin.

"You take the skin for six," Yipee offered. "It's good for you; you don't fight and you don't skin. Four dollars just to carry it where you go already. Very good."

"Yeah, I heard about you Chinee." The skin-collector drank again. "Live together like rats just to save a penny." He took another drink and got some on his shirt.

Yipee raised his hands. "All right, you don't buy; it's all right."

"Yeah, I don't buy," the skin-collector mumbled. It seemed like he had forgotten that Na-tio and Yipee were there, but he kept on talking. "Maybe I'll skin you, instead."

HORSES

I dropped my hands and sat back on my bundle. This foreigner was like Teacher—he drank too much whiskey. Would he jump up and start throwing things? Impossible to know.

Everyone was quiet for a long while.

"I know a wolf trap." Na-tio's voice made me jump. The foreigner opened his eyes.

"Who's gonna tell a story?" he demanded. "Longtime I ain't heardastory." It was difficult to understand what he said.

"This is a story," Na-tio replied. "I know this trap for Coyote or Wolf. The trap is old, from old time before. We do not make this trap now." He stopped staring at the fire and turned to the foreigner. "It is a story."

The foreigner grunted and scratched himself.

"This trap is of wood, stone, what you can find. You make ..." Na-tio's hands flew in the air. "... trap, a place, for the coyote. Big for Wolf."

Then he was quiet.

Was that the story?

Na-tio turned his face to the dark sky and pursed his lips. "Food brings Coyote—or Wolf—and ..." He sighed and shook his head. The foreigner made a snuffing noise. Or was it a snore?

Finally, Na-tio clapped his hands together and stretched out his arms, one flat on top of the other.

"Big wood, tree, see?" he raised the top arm high and shook it. "Animal goes to house for food but—"

Smash! Down crashed the tree-arm, onto the other. "Trapped and broken. People come and take Wolf or Coyote."

The foreigner stirred to speak but Na-tio hurried on. "The story is this:

"One time the people can hear crying. Someone is in the trap! Oh, no, where is little girl? The mother run, the people run, but she is broken. The little girl played in the trap—she took the food—and it fell. Because she did not know, the trap fell on her."

The foreigner laughed.

"The people were sad," Na-tio told him.

"Is it a true story?" I asked. All Crooked Mah's stories were true, no matter how old.

"Yes, true," Na-tio said.

"Hey!" The foreigner waved his bottle at the both of us. It was nearly empty. "Who drank all my whiskey?"

In fact, he had tipped the bottle over. The dogs had been lapping at the puddle and the neck of the bottle and were now asleep. But the foreigner hadn't noticed.

He turned the bottle upside down into his mouth, let it drop to the ground, and then slumped over, just like his dogs.

He pulled his wolf skin over his head and was quiet.

Na-tio sat very still. The foreigner began to snore, loud and steady.

I let out my breath.

Na-tio rose and moved around to the back of the tent. I followed.

He was tying the foreigner's horses to a lead—he was going to steal the horses!

I rushed to him. "Stop ... no ... you must not!"

"You may have one," he gestured over the three, offering my choice.

"I work for my things!" I hissed at him. Crooked Mah and the others never stole, no matter how poor or hungry they were. It was wrong to steal, they said.

"You don't want, I keep." He pushed me back and saddled his horse.

"You must not take the foreigner's horses!" I kept my voice low. That big foreigner and his dogs must not wake up to see this! Without horses, he'd have no transport, no one to carry his skins. This was not right!

Na-tio had finished packing his horse and was saddling up Blackie. I ran over and took the reins—Blackie was mine!

"The foreigner needs his horses, like we do," I tried. "For his packs, to do his work."

Na-tio was ready to go. The horses waited. What could I do? What would Crooked Mah say if he knew I was stealing!

Na-tio mounted. He clicked at his horse and they turned away. He waited again.

I shouldn't follow him; I must try to make him see.

He turned his head and looked down at me. "You go to the skins."

Now he wanted those horrible skins?

"He collects more than Wolf," Na-tio said. "You look, you can see better this time."

Was he trying to send me away so he could take Blackie?

"You go," he urged. "I wait."

It was dark. The shadows of skins dangled from their snouts. What was I supposed to see? I stepped in even closer. Wait, some of the tails were wrong, like horse tails. No, not horse, they were ... hair?

There were more, in a stack by the tree. I picked one up. It was hair, loose and silky at one end, tangled and gummy toward the other.

Oh! It was skin—curled and crisp. It was people hair—it was a scalp! The foreigner wasn't just skinning wolves, he was skinning

RAQUEL RIVERA

people, too. My head tingled, as if the foreigner was right behind me—pulling on my braid again.

"Nice hair," he'd said.

I dropped the scalp and ran to Blackie. I climbed up, kicked her sides, and took off.

I let the reins go loose, hanging onto the saddle with one hand. I rubbed the other hand along my trousers, but I couldn't rub away the tickle-feeling from those curling edges of scalp. Nasty shivers kept running across my head.

"Nice hair," he'd said.

"Maybe I'll skin you," he'd said.

I gave Blackie my heels again and again—we had to escape.

Behind me, I heard Na-tio and the horses—*kwa-lub, kwa-lub*—thudding over the soft ground. It was a good sound.

We rode for a long while in the dark. Blackie went slower now, picking her way among the rocks. I was tired but I wanted to be still farther from the skin-collector. That is what Na-tio called him.

Maybe the skin-collector was a demon. I kept this idea to myself; Na-tio might think I was bad luck, bringing demons on him.

"He trade money for skins," Na-tio said when we finally camped down under our blankets. We had made a big fire; the night was cold.

"Wolf skin and people skin, too." His blanket muffled his voice.

"He sells the scalps?" I protested.

Na-tio sat up and squinted. "He does not hunt the good way." His hands flew through the air. How I wished those hands could talk! Finally, he smoothed a spot on the ground next to his blanket. He picked up a stick.

"We are many on this land, long before the Anglos came." He drew a shape on the ground and touched it with his stick. "This is where my people love most—we travel here. Best place."

He drew a line up. "This, people-who-weave-blankets, sometimes friend, sometimes fight; they keep sheep."

"This," he drew a line across. "We always fight; these never friends. These," Na-tio drew many lines from the place, like the rays of the sun. "These are my people, too. We know and trade. We friend, marry, and share war." Then he drew a line straight down. "Mexican. Always war and raid Mexican."

I leaned over the drawing. What was Na-tio trying to tell me?

"I don't know where the Anglos fit." Na-tio's stick hovered over all the people he had shown. "Selling scalps," he shook his head, "is not hunting or war. I don't know it."

Na-tio jammed the stick into the ground. Then he scratched at his drawing until it was gone.

I rubbed my head, pushing through my hair to feel my own skin. It was good we had escaped.

Na-tio's horse was stamping. Na-tio turned and said something—soft, low ripples I didn't understand. The horse went quiet. Blackie was dozing. The new horses browsed the bushes.

And now I was a thief.

But I was glad to be with Na-tio; traveling was better this way. Na-tio had saved me and Blackie. If that made me a thief, I supposed that's how it was.

This made me think: if I could be a thief without wanting or trying, then maybe the skin-collector was no demon at all. Maybe he was just ordinary like me.

"I don't know," Na-tio repeated. "Skin-collector does not hunt the right way. He wastes the wolf skin. Taking scalps happens in war, not for money." He lay down, pulling his blanket around his shoulders. "He will fall sick, die maybe. It is good we leave." Na-tio fell asleep.

This was my chance to take a bath. I hadn't bathed since before the wolf attacked us—I was as grimy as Na-tio. But I was too tired; even my thoughts were blurry.

I was meeting the strangest people on the way to Prescott.

YIPEE

They had staked the new horses short so they would not try to run away. Two were quiet but not the Paint. He was the smallest and bushiest of the bunch—born wild. Yipee wanted to ride that Paint. He liked the coat. "Many colors—so cheering," he said as he brushed down the little horse's bristling hair.

"You must learn to like dark horses," Na-tio told him. "That white you ride—and this one—they show on the land forever. They will give you away."

Yipee shrugged and gathered the reins, along with a clump of the animal's mane down at the withers.

"Lift me?" he asked. "I don't want a saddle." Na-tio couldn't help smiling; Yipee's face was spilling light—that little horse was making him happy now. And he had not wanted to take it before!

Na-tio made a stirrup with his hands and braced himself. Yipee stepped, light as nothing, into Na-tio's hands and lifted himself onto the Paint.

Na-tio jumped away as the Paint gave a startled snort and bucked at the new weight on his back. Yipee held his place and chattered, soft and low. The Paint took a few steps back and then bolted.

Yipee held on by the mane, keeping the reins loose, and the Paint's nose went forward. He broke into a real gallop, trying to run from the creature on his back.

Yipee pulled the reins a little. The Paint didn't even know he was making big turns around the meadow. The sun flashed off the red, yellow, and white splashes on the horse's rump. Yipee was the right size to ride this strong little animal.

That Paint, he kept trying to shake Yipee off his back; he must have been used only as a packhorse before now.

But Yipee rode well—and the horse was learning this. Yipee let him have his lead for a while and then took him down to a comfortable lope, around and around the meadow. The Paint tossed his head, this way and that. His coat bristled with nerves, but he was listening.

Yipee took him down to a walk. He leaned over and rubbed the Paint's shoulder, murmuring and giving long, hard strokes down the neck. They stopped by Na-tio; Yipee's smiling cheeks squeezed his eyes almost shut.

"You keep him," Na-tio said.

Yipee ducked his head. "I should not."

But when he slid down and led the horse to the others, he staked the Paint near his white.

"Blackie is quiet; you learn from her." Yipee stroked the nose of the white horse.

He called back to Na-tio, "I'm hungry!"

"We eat one of these!" Na-tio waved at their little herd.

Yipee scowled. Na-tio had to laugh.

"If you don't eat Horse, you must hunt," he said, moving for the trees. "There is Quail here, maybe. Do you eat Quail?"

Yipee ran a hand along the Paint's back. All the colors rippled in response. He pulled a twig from the horse's tail. He joined Na-tio by the trees.

"But I don't know how to catch," he said.

Na-tio showed Yipee how to make bird arrows, with crosspieces fitted and tied below the point. "If we only touch, this part will knock them down anyway," Na-tio explained.

Yipee didn't have a bow but he knew how to be quiet. Quail was easier to catch in the fog, not a bright day like today. But after a while, Yipee's saddle pack was full of feathered bodies. Sometime, when they were not so hungry, Na-tio would show Yipee how to shoot.

It took a while to pluck and clean the birds. They drove them onto two long sticks placed across the fire. Drops of fat sizzled on the coals. The smell made Na-tio's stomach growl.

They tore into the juicy bodies, stripping the small bones in a mouthful. They were delicious!

Na-tio was very full. He didn't want to travel further today, even though there was still light. This place was very pleasant. He had a good feeling here. And Yipee was good company—restful.

This was how raiding should be.

Yipee stretched out and folded his hands over his belly. His eyes closed. Yipee's eyelashes were like a deer's. There was a smear of quail grease shining on his round cheek.

The air was warm but a breeze washed over Na-tio's face. He removed the bandage from his head. The fresh air blew a tingling feeling across his scalp. He hadn't eaten such a feast in a long while. He hadn't felt so comfortable. Na-tio's eyes drifted shut. The glug-glug of a creek sounded at the bottom of the slope. The crickets sang.

When he woke, the air had cooled. He had spotted the green shoots of a tea-bush earlier, just as he'd been falling asleep. He would show Yipee how to make good chai from this plant.

But Yipee was awake and moving around already. What was he doing?

Na-tio pretended to sleep while Yipee stirred up the fire and hung his kettle over it. Watching him squatting there, Na-tio remembered when he first spied on Yipee. Today the white hat was off—tossed onto a bush. Yipee's hair on top was bristly, like a porcupine. Na-tio wanted to brush his hand across it.

He kept his eyelids low so he could spy again. As the kettle steamed, Yipee rummaged through his pack. He pulled something out—Na-tio couldn't see without giving himself away.

Yipee picked up his pail and kettle and walked away. Strange.

Na-tio tracked him to the creek.

He found Yipee scooping water with his pail. He poured steaming water from the kettle. He touched the pail-water with his fingers and then added more kettle water. He rubbed his hands over a little yellow stone—it made suds, like yucca suds! Yipee was going to wash his hair!

But wait, he was taking off his clothes. He was going swimming. But surely he knew that one should swim in the morning, when the water was very cold. No wonder he was not so strong.

But wait—

Wait—what was this?

Na-tio heard his own breath huffing, ragged, from his open throat. He clamped down on it. He must not be heard.

He watched as Yipee scrubbed every part with the suds, from the porcupine bristles on top, all the way down.

He knew it! He had seen it that first night by the fire: the soft face, the narrow back! Well, he had suspected something; he remembered that now.

And now he saw it again—it was before his eyes! Yipee's round bottom, her smooth limbs—Yipee was a girl!

Na-tio was stuck. He watched as Yipee splashed off the suds. Hopping and huffing, she smacked her clothes against a tree.

She looked very strange.

It was possibly the most beautiful thing he had ever seen.

He blinked as she climbed back into her disguise. She combed her dripping, heavy hair with her fingers.

He knew it! He had known it! Well, almost. But so many other things had happened and he had forgotten to be suspicious.

She re-tied her braid, nice and smooth. She took up her things and walked back into the trees; all her soft curves were hidden again.

Na-tio shook himself and stumbled after her, back to the fire.

She must have dropped her pail and kettle. Na-tio could hear them clatter. They rolled down the slope in his direction. He picked them up for her.

She turned on him. "You peeked!"

"You cheated!" Na-tio exclaimed.

"I did not!" Yipee had gone pale.

She turned in circles, pulling at the shorter hairs on top of her head. "I did not cheat!" she kept saying, louder and louder, turning around and around.

She was going to make herself dizzy. "I did not, I did not—I survived!" She stopped. She began to shake—very hard. Was it a fit? She was talking low, not in English—jabbering.

Well, Na-tio hadn't meant to see her. Well, yes he had. But he hadn't been thinking to find a secret. Or had he?

Her talking got louder, then quiet again. She kept her back to him; she was shaking too hard. Would she fall down?

He'd been taught respect between brothers and sisters, between in-laws. It must be the same with her people. Look at her—she would be ill if she didn't stop this!

It was Na-tio's fault; he had done this.

He must do something—he'd try to make it right.

"Hey!" he called to her, sharp, so she would see, but she murmured on.

"Look here, it's only me, Na-tio!'

She raised her head and turned wide, blank eyes to him. Then she saw.

Na-tio had taken off his deerskin shirt, his leggings, and even his breechcloth. Now they were even.

Now she was staring. Well, he could bear it.

He would just watch her face as she looked up and down. And up again.

Was this enough—how long had he seen her? Was he starting to tremble?

Na-tio raised his arms and made a slow turn, all the way around.

RAQUEL RIVERA

Yipee bit the inside of her cheek. Then her eyes crinkled. She covered her face and turned away.

"Please put back clothes, Na-tio," she said. Which he did, quickly.

But she had stopped shaking, so he must have done right.

Na-tio cut stalks from the tea-bush and ran back to the creek for water to boil. Yipee helped to strip the long juicy needles from their stems.

She shivered while waiting for the water to boil, so Na-tio dropped his blanket on her shoulders. She gathered it to her.

"You are made straight and strong," she said, her eyes fixed to the fire.

"This is because my mother told me to swim in the morning, when the water is cold." Na-tio thought Yipee should know this, particularly.

"I was told to stay clean, eat fresh food, and boil water to drink tea," Yipee said. "Crooked Mah said it would keep me strong."

"Your mother?" Na-tio asked.

"Crooked Mah looked after me." Yipee nodded. "Like mother. Like father. That was the important thing, he said."

"You are grown now," Na-tio said, and the picture of Yipee by the stream came back to his eyes.

Yipee pulled the blanket tighter but she nodded again.

"Yes, I am grown. That is the important thing."

Yipee told the stories that night. She spoke of big cities, and gold, and railway tracks, and her Crooked Mah. Na-tio didn't understand everything she said, she talked so fast; sometimes it did not even sound like English words. Chinese, maybe.

He made more chai.

"Mmmm," he kept saying, to show he was listening. As the stars blinked open—one, then another, then many, then more—Na-tio nodded and nodded, "Mmmm."

Finally, they both drifted off.

CHAPTER

⇒ 12 ⇐

DARK NIGHT

I slept very hard that night; I was so tired. But when I woke up, it was still dark. I poked at the coals and put on a new branch. Little flames flickered. Na-tio was a hump under his blanket. The hump rose and fell.

Should I sneak away, now that he knew my secret?

Crooked Mah had hidden me all my life; and now I had messed it up.

I had even thought I really was a boy, until I got older and Crooked Mah explained how things were. This Gold Mountain, this country, was no place for a child—for a girl child, especially. There was danger everywhere, in the mountains and in the cities.

"I can keep you safe if you are a boy," Crooked Mah promised. "It is our best chance." I kept my braid long and my head shaved. Our traditional loose clothing hid me well. We changed jobs: a season of fieldwork, then a season in the mines, then a season doing laundry. There was even a short time in a Chinese food restaurant, before Crooked Mah decided that the hours were unhealthy for a growing boy.

As the years went on, he kept me young to explain my soft face and high voice. "It's your birthday; you are growing young again," he'd joke, pretending we were foreigners, with their custom of celebrating the date they were born. Then we would move on to the next place.

Na-tio was sleeping; now was a good time to sneak away. But would Na-tio track me? Would he chase me?

This was how I'd sneaked away from the railroad, too—late at night in the dark.

After Crooked Mah had died, I'd kept to myself. I was very sad and everyone left me alone. No one even teased me about my private bath. Maybe we were all sad. I suppose people were used to my ways. I suppose even I thought I was a kind of boy, even in my bath.

But I continued my English lessons. Crooked Mah had said it was my best chance, and he was right. When I carried bucket after bucket of mountain stone, I murmured the new words I'd learned during my last lesson. "Mister Brown resides in town," and "Mary, Mary, quite contrary," I would recite, while I shoveled snow, dirt, and sand.

RAQUEL RIVERA

The days became warmer and the snow melted. I felt unwell; my head ached and my stomach churned. Was I getting the dysentery?

At the Saturday night English lesson, my headache was especially bad.

"Have a drink with me," Teacher said, as he always did. This time I said, "Yes, please," as I took my place in the other chair.

Teacher laughed and slid the bottle across the table to me.

I took a sip. It warmed me, so I took a gulp. Teacher whistled. He packed his pipe and lit a match against his boot.

"We'll make an American out of you yet," he mumbled through his pipe as he puffed to get the smoke going.

"I am American."

It must have been the drink that made such a strange thing pop out of my mouth. I hadn't thought of it before, but I had no one in China; Crooked Mah had always told me this. I had no father and my mother died when I was born. I was not supposed to be there, Crooked Mah said, but I was. So he hid me, and I was quiet in his bundle as he walked the board off the boat into San Francisco. And he kept me. Now he was dead, too.

Teacher's eyes narrowed and he blew smoke. I coughed.

"Don't get above yourself." He tapped on the newspaper where he wanted me to begin reading. Then he pulled the whiskey out of my reach.

I read the headline: "*The Twin Mountains.*"

"Out of the midst of the beautiful Lake Nic– Nicara–"

"Lake Nicaragua." Teacher puffed his pipe.

"–Lake Nicaragua spring two magnificent pyramids, clad in the softest and richest green, all flecked with shadow and sunshine, whose summits pierce the billowy clouds."

Teacher loved this part of the paper. Every week this distinguished traveler wrote to the newspaper about his adventures. When he wrote about people, he was mean but very funny–Teacher would snort and laugh and sometimes explain the joke. But when the traveler wrote about the new places he saw, Teacher leaned back and closed his eyes, like he was doing now.

"They look so isolated from the world and its turmoil–so tranquil, so dreamy, so steeped in slumber and eternal repose." I understood "slumber," and "steeped" was like tea. Maybe the rest would become clear later on.

"These mountains seem to have no level ground at their bases, but rise abruptly from the water. There is nothing rugged about them–they are shapely and symmetrical, and all their outlines are soft, rounded, and regular. The highest being the furthest removed makes them look like twins. When not a cloud is visible elsewhere in the heavens, their tall summits are magnificently draped with them. They are extinct volcanos and consequently their soil (decomposed lava) is wonderfully fertile.

They are well stocked with cattle ranches, and with corn, coffee, and tobacco farms."

I was out of breath. I would have liked another drink, but the whiskey in the bottle was already low.

But Teacher was not sad or angry; he wasn't thinking of that woman Maddy. He was too interested to hear the story in the paper.

"You following any of this, Yee?" Teacher said, pushing the bottle back my way. "That Mark Twain must be the best reporter in these United States and Territories—makes me want to travel Panama-way myself!" His head wobbled and he smiled at me.

I took a gulp and passed it back. I was feeling good, too. My headache was gone.

"Maybe you are American, after all." He let his hand drop onto the table with a thump. "Hell, you drink like an American!" He swept his hand to the side, knocking the bottle so it rolled right off the table and onto the floor.

I jumped up and chased it across the room. Bottle in hand, I stood up and turned back. Teacher was staring at me, his mouth open, blurry eyes wide.

Then I felt it—the cold slap of wet trousers against my leg. How had I gotten so wet? I looked at the chair—we both did. There was a smear of blood on the seat. Was that my blood? I felt at the seat of my trousers.

Teacher pushed his chair back and stumbled over to me. He leaned in and I felt his warm breath.

"I'll be damned," he whispered. He leaned down, put his hand on me, and found a small, swollen breast.

I'd been discovered!

Of course, Crooked Mah had warned me—but that was so long ago! Nothing ever happened—I was kind of a boy, after all. Now, suddenly, I had turned into a woman—and Teacher knew it!

It all happened too fast. His hand was resting on my chest. His face was too close—he was breathing in my breath!

I didn't think—it was my arm, my arm just did it. The heavy bottle hit his head and he fell forward. It was only a tap—the bottle didn't even break! I stepped back before his dead weight knocked me down.

He slumped to the floor. I'd been discovered!

This was no place for a woman. All these months, stuck in the mountains. I'd heard the men talk—Chinese and foreigners both—they were animals. They'd tear me apart as soon as they knew—I must think!

I laid Teacher out as comfortable as possible—he was too big for me to pull onto the cot.

I put the empty bottle in his hand.

I would leave—that's all. I had no choice now. It was my best chance. I was lucky the snow had melted.

I wiped the bloody seat with my sleeve. Teacher had drunk so much, maybe he wouldn't remember this.

I left the shack. Tomorrow was Sunday. My work crew would notice, but it would be another day before the bosses learned I was gone.

I sneaked back to our site to get some things. What a mess I was! I took my change of clothing. I would tear up the extra shirt for rags to keep in my underpants.

What a bother it all was! Crooked Mah had warned me this would happen one day, and that it meant I was grown. At the time, it was just another one of his stories.

I took my things to the stream. I wouldn't wake anyone here. I shivered as I wrung out my bloody trousers. I made a bundle and started walking down. Lions and wolves hunted these mountains—what if they smelled my blood?

The fire crackled and Na-tio turned over. Was he awake? The sky was getting lighter—if I was leaving, I should go now.

But I didn't move.

I didn't want to leave this time; maybe it was all right to be discovered. I don't know why, but this idea made me smile.

"Today we bring the horses to my camp. It is not far." Na-tio sat up, rubbing his eyes. "You will smile there, too; you will meet many good horses at my camp."

He scratched his head until his hair stood up. He kicked off his twisted blankets and turned to the kettle. "Any more chai?"

SOLDIERS

Yipee rode her white horse and Na-tio was on his favorite. The others followed behind. They were a herd now.

Na-tio had been leading, faster and faster. The closer he got to camp, the more he wanted to be there already. It was like there were insects jumping in his belly and they wouldn't go away. Not until he found out what people would do when he returned—what would they say?

"We will see everyone soon," Na-tio assured Yipee. "You will see my mother." Maybe Father and Uncle and the others would be back from raiding. Na-tio chewed on the inside of his cheek. There was a bump there from all his chewing.

But it was time to return; he had horses now. He had raided something. He would take Yipee to Prescott as soon as this was done—he'd promised her this.

"Will your mother be angry that I am a stranger?" Yipee asked.

RAQUEL RIVERA

Na-tio raised his eyebrows. "Angry? Nooo," he considered. "But you are not family, not clan." He went back to chewing his cheek. "You are not prisoner. She will say, 'Where does this person sleep?'" Na-tio pursed his lips. "She does not speak Anglo–English–like Father and I do, but she will be kind if I bring you."

Na-tio was fairly certain of this.

"What is her house like?" Yipee asked. "Is she pretty?"

"Mmmm." When Mother smiled, she was pretty. But she didn't smile too much. That was her way.

Na-tio glanced back at Yipee. She kept urging her horse forward, but the trail was too narrow to ride side by side, so she'd fall back.

"Does she look after your brothers and sisters?" She crowded up again. Na-tio's horse was going to kick.

And Na-tio didn't know how to answer so many questions. He didn't have brothers and sisters. But Mother had cared for many children since Na-tio could remember. Dil-hee had been a baby when Mother adopted him; his real mother had died with Dil-hee's twin stuck in her. Dil-hee had stayed with them a long while until his grandmother asked to have him back, so Mother had to give him.

Then there was the time when Na-tio was little and Big Sister came to live with them. Big Sister was almost grown, but she needed a family until a husband could be found for her.

Big Sister had played with Na-tio and watched him, too. "Be careful!" she'd call to him when he climbed to the highest branches, gathering pine seeds for her basket. Everyone saw how capable she was, and soon she was someone's wife.

"No brothers and sisters," Na-tio told Yipee. "Mother cares for me and Father. Mother is second wife. First wife and children are gone. Now it is Mother and me."

"Where did they go, first wife and the children?" Yipee asked.

Na-tio frowned. "Go? They are dead." Where else would they be?

It seemed to Na-tio he had always known how Uncle's elder sister was Father's wife when Uncle and Mother were still young. Later, much later, Father married Mother. But until the cabin, nobody ever talked about what happened to First Wife and the children. Now Na-tio understood that the Anglo had murdered them. That he had taken their scalps—like the skin-collector. That was what Father had said. But Na-tio didn't want to think about that cabin ever again. He shook the memory off his shoulders, like it was a pesky fly.

Of course, he wouldn't tell any of this to Yipee. The dead might come if you spoke of them. They might think you were calling for them. Na-tio understood this—but Yipee asked so many questions.

And there she was, starting up again: "I suppose they won't mind that I am with you?" Moving forward, falling back, Yipee was acting like a nervous horse.

Na-tio tried to find the right words. "They will be happy to know you."

Was that correct? He didn't know how to say it. They will be interested. They will wonder at her face and hair, at her Anglo clothing and things. They will think that she is his wife, maybe.

Na-tio hadn't really thought this through. Why did he bring Yipee with him—why not send her to Prescott and be on his way again?

He started a new bump inside his other cheek.

Would everyone be kind to her? Mother had welcomed people before; she'd made a place for them in her family, hadn't she? Now Na-tio had another worry to chew on.

And what if Father, Uncle, and the chief had returned? Na-tio slowed his horse. He had been disobedient—he hadn't been learning well. What would the warriors do to him? He slowed his horse a little more. Maybe it was best to turn straight for Prescott after all.

"Na-tio, are you ill?" There she was, bumping into his horse again—asking questions again!

Na-tio scowled at her, then put his mouth into a straight, hard line. She would be quiet now, maybe—he needed to think. But then those insects in his belly started jumping again.

Knife and Awl, a real warrior would do as he pleased! Na-tio would not be afraid—he'd go straight to camp! Yipee, Father, and the rest of them could do what they wanted about that.

He dug his heels into his horse and bolted forward, leaving

Yipee and the other horses to catch up as best they could.

They wanted to reach camp before nightfall, didn't they?

Everyone's horses pastured in this low meadow, out of sight. But now they were gone. Tracks showed they had stampeded—or been driven away.

Na-tio put his hand across his mouth to show Yipee that she must be quiet. He tied his horse to a tree and gestured for her to do the same. They tied all their horses this way. They must sneak to camp on foot.

The smell washed over him first—the sharp smell of blood and body parts—and then he saw.

The widow's daughter lay face down, with a bullet hole in her back. Her shoulder and rib bones poked through torn muscle and skin; Coyote had been here, too.

Na-tio rushed through camp, searching all the dwellings. The di-yin was lying under the deerskin Mother had given for Na-tio's training. Now there was a black, clotted hole in it—a hole made by a bayonet.

Na-tio ran up the hill. He saw the chief's wife under a bush. The body was starting to swell.

Who did this? Where was Mother?

He followed the tracks further up the slope. He followed the blood.

RAQUEL RIVERA

Had Mother and the rest of them made it to the cave? Had Father and the warriors returned?

Na-tio looked down on the camp. Yipee was the only one standing, the only one moving—turning around from one body to the next.

Where was Mother? And the others—there were still others. They must have made it to the cave!

He scrambled up the hidden path. Gunshot and stab wounds— there were no arrows, no axe-wounds. The killers were soldiers, then—must be. The Anglo soldiers from the fort. But why?

The cave was a hiding place—good as any fort. Soldiers didn't fight well in the hills. They stood still and shot their guns together, at one time. Some guns were so big that horses pulled them on wheels. Na-tio had seen these. They were powerful guns but ridiculous on a hill.

The pass to the cave had no place for a troop to stand still and shoot together. They must fight on their own, the way people did.

Na-tio ran higher. Mother was a good shot; she and the others could kill many soldiers from high ground like this. They could roll boulders down on them. The soldiers must have given up and gone away.

"Na-tio!" Yipee was running up, but he couldn't wait.

Oh! The widow lay across the path. She had a musket-ball hole in her belly; a raven was pulling a strand of shiny nerve from the wound. The bird shrieked at Na-tio and flapped away. Anglo soldiers had never bothered his family before. What new war was this?

"Ah-oh!" Yipee was shouting. He looked back; she had stumbled over a small foot in a deerskin moccasin—the chief's son!

Na-tio heard a sound in his own throat. He had to get to the cave; the rest would surely be safe in the cave. He was nearly there.

No!

The cave was gone—it was blocked by rocks!

He tore at them.

"Mother!" he shouted. "Mother! Are you in there?"

Those soldiers, those bad-smelling, hairy-faced betrayers must have done this somehow!

"Here, over here!" Yipee was pulling smaller rocks off the pile. Na-tio rushed to her and together they managed to move the big one. It thundered down the slope, crushing bushes.

"Mother!" Na-tio called through a small crack in the stones. He had to find a way in.

"Be careful," Yipee said. "Or the rocks will roll and crush us."

If he could shift this heavy stone, there might be enough space to crawl through.

Na-tio grunted, pulling until his head felt like it would burst. Yipee cleared small rocks, making room for the heavy rock to loosen.

It moved!

Yipee pushed from one side. Na-tio pulled.

"Let me." Na-tio took her place and put all his weight behind it. She pulled. His feet slid out from under him. It was no use. He looked for a sharp rock.

Na-tio's grunts filled his ears—loud and long, like cries. He hacked into the ground through the soft, slipping pebbles. It was so hot. He couldn't see.

"Mother," he croaked. "I'm coming."

He dug his toes into the pit he had dug.

Yipee had found a rope. She wrapped it around the big rock and tied it.

There was a shout; Na-tio didn't recognize his own voice. He grunted and shouted as he pushed against the rock and let it roll back—push, roll, push, roll.

Yipee stopped pulling. "Na-tio, wait. I will get help. You must stop—you will be hurt."

Na-tio couldn't hear much. The world had gone hazy.

"I will come back." Yipee ran down the slope. She picked her way on tiny feet, just like a mule. And then everything went black.

"Na-tio, drink." He heard his own name called—out loud. It must be important.

Yipee was holding his head in her gentle hands. He choked on the water she gave him and she wiped his face. He sat up.

He looked around. Oh, yes.

No!

"Mother!"

Na-tio turned back to the rock. The Paint was there, waiting to pull.

Na-tio got behind the rock again. Yipee urged the Paint forward. The horse drove its hooves into the soil and strained against the rock. Na-tio dug his moccasins into the ditch he'd made and pushed. Yipee ran around and pushed, too. The Paint's nostrils opened for more air. Na-tio's arms trembled but his legs held firm.

Tip, tip, tip—topple! The boulder rolled from its place and Yipee ran around to stop the Paint from straining any longer.

Now there was a small passage into the cave.

"Mother!" Na-tio called. "I'm here!"

The cave was cool and dark. The light through the passage did not reach far, but Na-tio could see bodies among the rocks, twisted and broken.

"Mother," he whispered. "Anyone here?"

"*Ehhh ...*"

What was that sound? That was someone. That was the sound of someone!

"I'm here," Na-tio assured the sound. "I will find you."

"*Eeehhh ...*" came the sound, quieter this time. It was by the cave wall, behind those rocks.

Na-tio climbed and the sound went sharp—"*Eeehh—eeee!*"

Oh, no, the person was under Na-tio! He rolled off the stones and dropped to the other side.

"Na-tio?" Yipee was calling through the small passage.

"I'm here—someone's here!" Na-tio called and dropped his voice. "Where are you?"

"Here ..." came the creaky voice just by his knees. Na-tio reached and felt fingers, a hand—he grasped it.

"Mother! I knew I would find you!" He pulled away stones and touched her soft hair, tangled with grit and sand.

"I knew you would come for me, Husband," came the dry, crumbly voice. "Did you bring our son? Did he do well?"

"Mother, it is me, Na-tio. I've come for you." Na-tio squeezed the hand. He stroked the hair.

"Their sticks touched the ground and made it jump. They made the hill fall to bury us ..."

Na-tio pulled away more rocks—careful, careful. His hand reached for her. She was all swollen and pulpy. He pulled back.

"Why did they kill us, my husband?" Na-tio felt faint breath on his hand.

"Mother, I'm Na-tio." Why wouldn't she understand this? He wiped tears off his face. He snuffled and stroked her hair some more. He was afraid to move another rock. She was already so crushed.

"My son? You are here, too?" Mother stirred her hand and found his kneeling leg. She made a funny sound, "*Eehhhh–hoch-hoch ...*" She patted his knee. And she stopped.

Na-tio's fingers searched for her mouth, her nose. There was no more warm air.

The cave had grown cold.

"Na-tio!" someone was calling.

Just a moment.

His head was too heavy to lift. His throat was blocked—he could not call. His heavy hand rested on Mother's face, but she was not there.

"Na-tio," came the voice, high and foreign.

There was the sound of crunching rocks. He heard a grunt, then a thump. There was a low sound in a language he did not know.

Someone was coming.

It wouldn't do any good. Everyone was dead in here.

"Na-tio!" the voice whispered. It sounded urgent. "Na-tio—*eeeak! Oh, ah!* Bodies—*ah!*"

"Na-tio—answer me!" the voice hissed in the dark.

He would speak, only his throat was blocked.

Then something landed on his shoulder, hard.

"Ha!" the voice cried. "I found you!" He was gripped and held. It was quite warm.

"We must go ...." The voice tickled his ear.

RAQUEL RIVERA

A great breath shook from his belly. His throat cracked and loosened.

"This is my mother," he told the voice.

"They must have used nitro," the voice said. "They blasted the mountain, just like on the rails."

He turned, even though it was too dark to see. It was Yipee. Yipee had come to visit him and Mother.

She took his hand. "We must go."

"But why did they kill us all?" Na-tio asked. "Why did they kill my mother?"

"If you don't speak English to me, Na-tio, I don't know what you are saying."

CHAPTER

⇒ 14 ⇐

TALK, TALK

I had to pull Na-tio from those rocks. I tried to explain as we went. I told him about Crooked Mah, that he had been buried, too. I kept talking into his ear. "It was snow that time," I said, "but the mountain fell, just the same." I don't know what nonsense I said. I had to get him out—out of the rocks, away from the bodies.

In the dark cave, I blinked away the old pictures—the snow, the bright, the shine, the hard, frozen bodies—not like the crushed bodies we climbed over now.

"Not us," I kept saying. "We are not buried."

Na-tio's hand was cold, even though we were outside now, in the sun. His skin fell loose from his face. He stooped; he looked old. The Paint was nervous and spooky; his eyes rolled and he was blowing hard. He jerked and danced, making it difficult to untie him. Many angry ghosts must have flown from the cave when we opened the rock.

We all had to get away from this place.

Na-tio wanted to go after the soldiers. Elders, women, and children had been killed; they must be avenged. Na-tio held himself straight now. He pursed his lips in the direction of their trail. "They go to the fort, maybe."

The Paint and the others carried food from the camp: seeds that had been ground up for flour, dried deer meat, and sheets of dried fruit or vegetable. But most of the stores—and the people's tools, baskets, water jugs, everything—Na-tio had insisted be burned, along with all the dwellings.

In one hut I'd found a beautiful blanket. It was so fine, made with such bright, cheerful colors. It was a shame and a waste to burn something so pretty and well made. I bundled it up and hid it among my own things. If Na-tio didn't want it, he could trade it for something good later when he calmed down. He looked very fierce now.

But that was better than the gray, hunched boy who had been dragged out of the cave yesterday. And it was much better than he had been during last night's horrible burning: Na-tio had screeched like an eagle getting its wing ripped off. He'd wailed like a ghost. I worried he might throw himself into the fire.

This morning he was himself again—except with a new, hard glint in his eyes. "Maybe we should let the soldiers go," I tried.

"We cannot fight them all and their fort."

Na-tio kept his horse to the trail. Blackie shifted under me.

"I can fight." Na-tio's eyes went black. His sharp nose pointed straight ahead. "I can die, but I can fight first."

He wasn't thinking right; I couldn't leave him like this. "You are not feeling well now. You wait—you will be strong again. You will decide later."

He wasn't even hearing me.

I shouted. "You said you would take me to Prescott!" I felt my face go hot; he did—he had promised me. Suddenly, I couldn't bear the thought of being on my own again. I didn't want him to go away from me.

Besides, I couldn't let him go to just be killed, could I?

He blinked and finally looked my way. He looked over the animals and the food packs we had bundled together.

"Please." I spoke soft this time. "You promised."

He slumped and let out a breath.

Na-tio turned his horse. "All right. I take you to Prescott."

CHAPTER

PRESCOTT

He was too tired. At first, anger had made Na-tio strong—ready to set the fort on fire. He had dreamed how it would pop and snap with the fat of burning soldiers. But as he led Yipee to Prescott, his bones started to feel weak. His fight was being pushed out by drooping muscles. At they entered the town, Na-tio couldn't even feel the reins in his hands.

It was ugly; it was trampled flat, no grazing. Prescott was dead ground. There was a long porch made of boards and a roof. There were tall dwellings behind it. There were glass windows, like in the cabin with the baby.

There were hairy-faced men who wore hard boots and tied their trousers with iron clasps. There were Anglo women wearing long tunics that dragged in the dust. Na-tio even thought he saw one of his own people—only this person did not wear deerskin and moccasins, but clothes like the others. If Na-tio was not feeling so unwell, he would have greeted him and asked why he chose Anglo clothes. There were no soldiers, which was good. Na-tio could not bear to see a soldier.

He blinked. The sunlight had been giving him headaches ever since he came out of the cave. The last time he was here, Prescott was only two small cabins that sold supplies to the miners who dug into the hills for gold metal. Father had traded at Prescott once, for a gun and bullets.

Now Na-tio squinted through the blowing dust. Yipee was tying the horses to a post.

She took a small rolled bundle off the Paint and held it in both arms, like it might break.

"Now we do business," she said, and led Na-tio through the biggest door.

At least it was darker in here. Na-tio rubbed his sore head.

Yipee was talking to the woman who stood behind a long cupboard. She wore her hair up in a pile; it was the color of sunset.

"You wanna tell your friend to stop staring?" she said to Yipee, but she smiled and fluttered her light eyes at him. Na-tio looked away.

Yipee placed her bundle on the cupboard and rested her hand on it. "We have something special, we sell for good price," she said.

"Honey, I ain't buying. I got something special for sale myself." The sunset woman leaned over her cupboard. The top of her tunic was so low, she semed to burst from its frilly edge. She wiped the cupboard with a wet rag. It shone so that Na-tio could see her pale arms in it.

"I can sell you boys a drink but I can't let you upstairs. The girls got the afternoon off."

"We have a fine blanket." Yipee patted the bundle. "Very warm, very good. We can sell at good price."

The woman shooed them away. "The general store is that way, honey. They might trade for wild goods." Yipee turned to leave.

Her boots clomped against the porch boards. Na-tio hurried to hold her back: what blanket? Why now did Yipee have a fine blanket? He took the bundle and peered into it.

"What is it, Na-tio?"

It was the widow's blanket. She had taken the widow's blanket—had she lost her mind? Na-tio stepped off the porch into the sunlight, the bundle safe under his arm.

The light blinded him. Terrible pains shot through his head.

He mustn't sit down; the Anglos mustn't see him weak.

"Na-tio, are you all right?" He felt Yipee's small hand on his arm, guiding him back into the shade of the porch.

Someone brushed against him, hard.

"Town's getting crowded with all types," he heard.

"Too many types, y'ask me," someone replied.

Yipee pulled on him and they went through another door. It was cooler inside.

The pain moved to the back of his head. He could see.

It was all guns. There were small ones, like the Anglos carried in their belts. There was a rifle like Father's, only this one was new. Its barrel shone blue in the dim light. Na-tio could kill better with a rifle. Soldiers died faster from a rifle.

"Pa-ah!" Here, too, there was a girl behind a long cupboard. Her pale hair fluffed like feathers. "There's some Indians want to trade!"

"No, excuse me, it is a mistake," Yipee was saying as an Anglo came out from the back, pulling crumbs from his beard.

"I see that rifle." Na-tio pursed his lips in the direction of the long, pretty weapon.

"I bet you do." The gun-man pushed at the girl and she scurried into the back, out of sight. Then he crossed his arms. He didn't move behind the cupboard and he didn't take the rifle down from the wall.

"That's a Winchester repeater—beautiful piece of machinery. It costs $29." He looked Na-tio up and down, then at Yipee. "You boys got $29?"

The bundle slipped away from Na-tio. Yipee was talking fast and unrolling the blanket on the gun-man's long cupboard.

"We have a special blanket. Very good work; this long wool only, you see? Special sheep my grandmother breeds. All people want her blankets."

Yipee smoothed the widow's blanket carefully, showing off the fine work on both sides. Of course it was fine work. The weaver had been skilled. The widow had traded a good horse for that blanket, to wear at her daughter's Changing Woman ceremony.

But Yipee had gone mad—it must be. What was this talk of grandmothers—this talk of selling? She would sell the things of his murdered family? She was a disgrace.

Na-tio would find a rifle the good way, not like this. He crossed to the cupboard, taking hold of the blanket. He started to roll it up again, but the gun-man put his hairy hand on it—he touched the widow's blanket!

"Here now, just hold onto your feathers ..." the gun-man began.

"No!" Na-tio's arms trembled as he tied the bundle together. His legs were shaking as he rushed for the door.

And that crazy Yipee was still talking: "Thank you, we think on this."

STORYTELLER

"Na-tio!" I looked for him up and down the porch. He was tying the bundle to his horse. I ran to him—he was acting strange. He glared at me.

"What is it?" I asked.

His eyes glittered into me. "You lied. You are a liar."

What? Why was he angry? I never did anything!

"You lied on your grandmother. You lied on the widow's blanket."

I was trying to help him! "You wanted the gun—how you get it if you don't pay?"

"Liar," he said.

"I was doing business. Nothing wrong with business," I huffed. I unhitched Blackie. Na-tio was mounting his horse. He was leaving.

That was fine—who needed him? I also had things to do. A liar, he called me!

"You steal horses and you call me a liar!" I whispered, because I knew what people did to horse thieves.

He looked down at me from his big horse, amazed.

"I took for my family—for those who cannot raid. They ask, I must give; that is the warrior way." His eyes were wide; his hands flew. "I gave you the Paint!"

He was so certain. But he didn't know anything about town. I knew how to do business. Crooked Mah and the others, they all made business—and they knew right from wrong!

I unhitched the Paint, tying his lead to Blackie's saddle. His warm, spotted flank twitched in the sun.

Na-tio did give me the Paint.

"It was a story!" I tried to explain, waving my arm at the row of shops and saloons. "Just for friendly talk and trade. He sees what he buys. I don't cheat." I lowered my voice to a whisper again. Cheat was another word that upset people very much.

Na-tio frowned. He closed his eyes and rubbed his head. "I don't know these stories," he said.

And he rode away. He rode away from me.

CHAPTER

17

THE GOOD HILL

Na-tio didn't travel far. He was tired; he needed to grow strong. As soon as he could, he tied the horses where they might graze and started climbing into the hills.

It was good to leave the flat, beaten ground of that town. Up here, among the pines, the strong wind blew all his head pains away.

So much had happened and now he was alone. He had done wrong things; this must be why.

The wind blew hard against him.

That cabin was where things began to go wrong; those Anglos, Father, the baby. One moment the baby was laughing at the colors of the curtains, and then Na-tio's arrow had slid through him, like he was water, or smoke. Na-tio didn't want to be a baby-killer; but it had happened.

He turned around under the big sky, watching the tops of the tall pines bend in the wind. He let out a long, shrill wail. He

RAQUEL RIVERA

shouted and howled until the back of his throat rang. It was right that he do this for his family who were gone.

Na-tio drove his fists into his eyes and rubbed hard. Before the spots had left his sight, he was running up—farther up. His legs pounded against the steepness, and still he was slow! He leaned forward and pushed with his hands, grabbing at brush and rock—higher, higher—until the spots in his eyes came back and he had no more breath to go on.

Never mind; he had run far enough.

Bent over, gasping, Na-tio put a hand to his head wound, which was hot and wet. He checked his fingers; there was no blood, only sweat.

He gazed down into the valley on the other side and at the next hill, and the hills beyond that. The wind gusted and sang in his ears. It pushed against him, but his deerskin tunic kept him comfortable. And the sun—the sun had finally stopped punishing him, giving him headaches. Now it warmed his face. He sat down on a lichen-covered rock.

He wanted Mother.

All at once she came back to him, large and warm. Her arm was around him—how small he must have been. Everyone was around the fire—it was dark and the stories had begun. Father was telling a story that night, just as he had learned it from his own grandfather. Everyone was quiet and still; Na-tio's eyelids kept falling. Mother was so comfortable to lean on, he drooped against her—into her warm smell, her breathing sides.

"Stay awake, Son." Her rough palm passed over his forehead, making him blink.

Faces danced around the fire: Father's, the other warriors, the women with children snoring in their arms. "Stay awake. Learn our stories so that you may live well and pass them on."

It wasn't like Mother to disrespect a story by speaking instead of listening. The idea must have come through her touch, her nature—herself.

Remembering this made something rip inside, tearing at Na-tio's throat, all the way down to where he sat. He almost toppled over.

Then another picture came from long ago. He was in a lean-to; they must have been traveling. Na-tio was small in this picture, too. In the dark, Father sat close behind Mother. They looked like seated shadows. Father's arm moved up to the crown of Mother's head then down, slow and smooth, all the length of her shiny hair. He was combing her hair. Mother's head bobbed gently under his strokes, her face raised to the night sky.

Na-tio took a small, careful breath, then another. The blowing wind kept him from falling. He did not rip apart. The wind gusted all around, holding him tight.

RAQUEL RIVERA

A young deer picked her way across the hilltop, nibbling at branches. She startled when she saw Na-tio and, in three high bounds, was down the hill and out of sight.

He could look for Father and Uncle—he could look for Father's family, who traveled the dry hills to the south. They would welcome him.

But Na-tio didn't want to move. The sun made him quiet as he thought of Mother and Father. The wind blew against him.

If only he had followed Father and Uncle, like a novice should.

No, if only he hadn't gone raiding at all—if only he'd stayed with Mother. He could have saved her, maybe. If Na-tio had been ready to raid, why was he now so lost and alone? He should fight the soldiers. He should go to war—make the soldiers pay with their own lives.

But could their lives pay for everything Na-tio had lost?

Na-tio slid down the rock, knocking his head along the way: it was best to knock out all these thoughts. What use were they?

It wasn't fair to attack women, children, and old people, to bury them in the mountain. It wasn't fair, the baby having to die. All these sudden moments, with no time for anyone to figure out a better way.

Sharp grasses tickled his bare neck and he brushed at them. Then he stopped thinking, and there was only sun and the bending pines.

The wind was cold now that the sun was low. Na-tio stirred himself from the ground. He should see to the horses. He should build a fire down below. He would camp here for now. He wouldn't think about anything else for now.

He scrambled back down on stiff legs. There were big trees by the dry creek that would provide him shelter for tonight. He would look for water tomorrow.

As he reached the bottom, Na-tio smelled fire.

He hurried to his horses.

They were fine: his favorite and the other two he had raided.

But what was this? The Paint was also with them ... and that white horse, too!

Yipee was crouched over a small flame, blowing sparks and feeding it dry leaves. She looked up.

"They want too much money for boarding and hay in Prescott." Her voice wobbled. "I suppose I can camp around here, too, if I want."

Na-tio smiled. "You came back."

THE NOVICE

"We got work!" I rode hard into camp and pulled Blackie to a stop.

Na-tio always stayed behind; he didn't like Prescott. Now he was leaning against a rock, throwing bones. He'd burnt the small bones black on one side—they were for games, like dice. He must have been betting against himself.

"They round up cattle—and all the new babies." I slid off Blackie's neck and let the reins drop over her nose. For so many days I had come back from town with nothing. Now, finally, there was good news. "We got work!"

The boss at Double Y Ranch had come into town, looking for help with spring roundup. I tried to tell the boss about my good work for Mrs. Hall but he'd said, "On account of you've got arms, legs, and a head to go with 'em, I can use you."

"The boss said I go to Double Y and they are looking for me," I told Na-tio. "They don't care I'm Chinese—Chinese, Indian, black man, Mexican, no matter, the boss says." I hopped on one foot, then the other, explaining it to Na-tio.

It was just as I had wanted!

Na-tio sat there, looking at me, shielding his eyes with one hand.

"You must come, too." I squatted down beside him.

Na-tio snorted. "I do not work Anglo ranch."

But this was real paying work—this was some luck for me! For Na-tio, too, if he wanted to understand. He wasn't doing much else, anyway—just moping around. Why couldn't he try it for a while? Then we could still be together.

"Nooo," I agreed. "But you told me you are only novice—"

Na-tio turned on me, glaring.

"—I only say that because you do ranch work for a while, learn things no other novice knows, maybe. Be a better warrior, maybe."

Na-tio took a long breath.

I held mine. Na-tio had camped here awhile already. He'd never mentioned soldiers or vengeance again. He hadn't talked much, really. He didn't seem to have anywhere to go. Maybe all his relatives had died in the cave.

Of course, he was sad. He seemed content to be alone in the hills most of the time. And he always brought something back to camp when he returned—deer, good plants, or firewood.

But this was our big chance; we could spend all day on horseback, doing useful work and getting paid for it, too.

"It is a big adventure," I suggested, "for the brave."

He shrugged.

I jumped up and pulled open my pack. I knew Na-tio admired my shirt, so I had them make up a length of red flannel at the general store. I could do this now that I would be making wages.

"This will look so well on you," I flapped the new shirt out and held it against him—it would fit.

"You try the ranch," I coaxed. "You don't like it, you leave." If Na-tio would try and see how good the life was, surely he would never want to leave.

Na-tio stroked the red flannel.

CHAPTER

🥀 19 🥀

DOUBLE Y

The owner of the Double Y Ranch had the face of a bird, so sharp and thin his eyes were almost on the side of his face. They found him in the stable, leaning over the back leg of a gelding.

"Put him in a stall for the week—see if a rest'll fix it up," he said to the other man, who was holding the horse's rope. The other man led the limping horse away.

The boss took off his hat. Na-tio and Yipee waited behind.

"We got two more come on, Mr. Holt." The boss scratched his head and stepped away.

The owner looked at Yipee. "Kinda small, don't you think, Mr. Bart?"

The boss shrugged, "I tried him with a rope—I tried 'em both, Mr. Holt. I reckon we need every hand we can get."

The owner squinted. "You Indians?"

"This one's Chinese, he says," the boss said.

RAQUEL RIVERA

"Chinese, hey? That's a new one. You Chinese, too?" The owner turned to Na-tio. Yipee had convinced him to put on his new red shirt, but he still wore his leggings. Now the owner was staring at his feet. They were comfortable in moccasins.

"No, sir, he's Indian," the boss said.

The lame horse whinnied. He didn't want to go in the stall.

Na-tio could feel the owner staring hard at him, but he kept his eyes on the other man, who was clucking and cursing as he slapped a set of reins against the horse's rump.

"He's a good Indian, Mr. Holt," the boss spoke up. "These two have been camping around Prescott for a while. Not a problem from either of them, by all accounts." He smacked his hat against his leg. "We are real pressed for hands, sir. I don't see as we can turn anyone away."

"That true?" The owner was still staring. "You a good Indian?"

Na-tio was very good, but this Anglo was rude to ask. Na-tio clamped down on his teeth. He nodded.

"What's your tribe?"

Keeping his voice even, Na-tio told him. The sound rippled like cool water off his tongue. It had been a long time since he had spoken his language out loud.

The owner and the boss looked at each other.

Yipee spoke up, eyes darting around the group. "He is good, very good. No worry for this. He save me—many times."

The owner shook his head and turned away from them all.

"Tell Cook to lay in supplies for two more." As he walked away, he raised his voice to carry. "They better know their way around a rope, Mr. Bart!"

Na-tio didn't like that owner much, but he could feel Yipee's joy tingling through his new red flannel shirt.

🐿 20 🐿

ROUNDUP

The sun hadn't even come up. About a dozen of us were shivering around Cook's fire—all the able men the boss could find for spring roundup. The boss himself was over by the temporary rope corral, with the owner and the wrangler. The horses were milling inside, nervous—fresh off their wild season on the range.

"You must eat," I urged Na-tio. "Too much work today."

Na-tio chewed but he looked like he was asleep.

"Everybody git their ride!" Shorty passed by, moving toward the corral, while we all shoved the last of the bacon and yesterday's biscuit into our stuffed cheeks.

Jack mounted and rode into the corral. As the best roper in the outfit, his first job was to cut out a horse for every hand.

"Don't you give me another tired nag," the buster complained. "I had to dig my spurs so deep in the last one, I near couldn't find 'em at day's end!" He laughed at his joke. The buster wasn't a real name. Everyone called him that because he always said he was the best bronc-buster he'd ever met. There wasn't a horse born he couldn't ride, he said.

But he was wrong about one thing: none of these horses was tired. They were spirited, and most of them didn't remember their training well. Blackie, the Paint, and the others were kept back at the ranch. Cowboys coddle their own horses. Mrs. Hall used to say it and now the boss said it, too.

Jack's horse was different, of course; they were a special team. They rode into the jumpy herd. Jack picked a horse and his mount knew just how to follow, stay close and fast, and not let their prey get away. Jack's rope always landed right. This time it slid down the neck of a big red horse. Little by little, the cutting team worked their way back with the red horse on a lead.

"Starfire will do you, I guess," Jack said to the buster, before turning back into the herd.

When I was given a mount, I slipped my saddle on his back. I had aired my saddle blanket overnight, and beat out the sweat and dust before breakfast. A horse will sit quieter if his saddle blanket doesn't hurt.

"*Hoo-eee!*" There were shouts and laughter from all the hands. The red horse looked silly: the buster's saddle now hung upside down, under his belly. The blanket was pushed up his neck. But he didn't look as silly as the buster, sitting in the dust.

RAQUEL RIVERA

I turned to Na-tio. He was already mounted, pulling the reins on his dancing horse. He shrugged. He was right: it wasn't so funny. Everyone gets thrown by a horse some time.

Jack brought a yellow mustang to the edge; it was led away by a waiting hand.

He looked down at the buster. "Too much horse for you?" he asked, very concerned.

The buster jumped up, twisted the saddle upright, and punched the horse's belly, hard. He pulled the saddle-straps tight, before the horse could puff out and trick him again.

All that morning, as we traveled to the next camping place, the buster fought with his horse. The red horse made sneaky bucks and sudden starts, while the buster was heavy on his spurs. The buster was hot and sweaty, and the day's work had not even begun. The other hands made jokes the whole time.

"That horse, he need more time to train. He liked the wild season too much," I said to Na-tio.

"That hand is not so good as he thinks," Na-tio replied.

It started to rain when we reached the next camping place. Cook set up a tarp over his wagon and fire. The day's roundup was finally beginning. Na-tio and I set off to cover our section. The rain got heavier and the wind blew hard. I tied my kerchief around my hat, under my chin. This was supposed to be the best part of the day—riding through the new country, before we had to turn back to camp, driving in all the cattle we found on the way.

But now the rain poured off my hat and ran down the front of my oilskin, over the horse's shoulders. I hated rain; it was like a cold bath.

"We will sleep on wet ground tonight," I complained, but Na-tio didn't hear me through the wind and the water.

On the way back, we found a cow stuck in a swollen creek. Her baby was crying; the rushing water kept knocking him off his skinny legs, but he wouldn't leave his mother's side.

Na-tio dismounted, took his rope from the saddle, and walked into the creek. He sank—up past his knees.

"There's mud!" he called. The water rushed around Na-tio, trying to sweep him under. I stared upstream—as if that might stop a flash flood. We had to get out of here. At any moment, this basin could become a channel for raging waters.

I threw my rope at the cow's head, but in my rush I got one horn only—damn! But the cow began wiggling her head this way and that, getting it through my lasso, like she understood.

Na-tio went after the calf. He tied the front legs and dragged it toward the shallows. The calf kicked and shouted but couldn't do much else, tied up like that.

The water was rising; the cow was now straining to keep her nose high. I wrapped my rope around the saddle horn and kicked

RAQUEL RIVERA

hard. The horse dug in and pulled. The cow was shouting over the rushing waters—the creek and the rain—and then her head went under.

From the bank, the calf struggled against Na-tio's rope, trying to return to Mother.

The horse's withers rippled under me. The footing was loose here; stones scrambled under hooves. I clucked and urged—then begged and bossed. The horse strained harder—how long had we been doing this? The water was higher still. A long tree branch came whooshing downstream and caught on my rope, almost pulling me and the horse in. Luckily, it snapped against a rock and the pieces washed away. Branches, stones, even a rusted old wheel, came hurtling down the creek. What if something had already smashed the cow? What if her legs were broken underwater? Should I cut my rope?

I looked for Na-tio, but he was pulling the calf onto high ground. If only the rain would stop pounding for a minute, so I could think! Was the cow drowned by now? Could I just let go and get out of this damned basin?

Then Na-tio saw me. He started pulling with his arms, as if he had my rope in his hands. Yes, that was it—I stopped urging the horse and twisted around to give the rope a sharp yank with both hands, then another. I felt something give. The cow must be alive because I could never move her dead weight—I must still try! The horse pulled; my arms were coming out of their sockets from tugging. Then the cow's nose rose out of the water, snorting and sneezing. She was coming fast now—she must have found stony ground. We all moved up, out of the basin. I leaned into the horse's neck, shouting praise through the thunder. We were free.

Na-tio was at the top. He loosened the ropes on the calf, who ran to his mother. We drove them both on.

CHAPTER

❧ 21 ❧

STARFIRE

"Get off," the wrangler's voice hissed in the night. Maybe he was talking to the horses in his pen.

Finally the rain had stopped. A big moon shone down. Na-tio and I had nighttime watch over the day herd—fat steers that were coming in for market, and the few cattle that had been found with other ranches' brands on their hides.

I was humming a nice song. The herd was always jumpy and, for some reason, a song helped keep them still. Even a little sound—the crack of a branch or a hooting owl—might set them to stampeding. Once a herd started to stampede, it was difficult business to get them to stop. People, horses, trees—everything got trampled under a stampede.

Jack told me how it was: once they start running, the only thing to do—after you've got your sorry hide out of the damn way, Jack said—is for some brave soul to ride out in front of the thundering herd and get right up to the lead animal. Then you beat on him until he turns the herd, and you get that herd running in circles until they wear themselves out. If not, they'll run straight forever—or until they drop into a canyon.

So Na-tio and I had to keep them quiet, and a song seemed to help.

Na-tio yawned. "We don't sleep, we will be weak."

"It is our turn." I sang my words so the cows would not be disturbed. "Others will watch tomorrow."

"That Jack doesn't watch nights," Na-tio said.

"He is the best roper," I sang. "We are only new."

The wrangler had pastured the horses some way off, but his voice came through the thin air again: "Get away, now. Get some sleep!" Who was he talking to?

I squinted. It was the buster—and the red horse. The horse was rearing, pulling against the buster's lead.

Na-tio raised his eyebrows. All through supper, hands had been bothering the buster about the red horse.

"Must have hired you for your looks," they laughed. "'Cause you sure can't ride!" They joked like that and the buster didn't like it. Now he must want to train the red horse, so he could boss him tomorrow and show everyone.

Na-tio and I rode in closer to watch. The wrangler pushed back his hat and crossed his arms.

"I can't go to bed 'til all the horses is corraled," he complained.

The buster had tied the horse to a stump. The horse ran, but he couldn't get away from the buster. He just ran around and around.

"Didn't like the marks on him when he come in," the wrangler rubbed his forehead. "The buster's too heavy with his heels and the quirt. He's gonna ruin that horse."

"He push too hard," Na-tio murmured.

"I think he is mean," I said.

"He'll make Starfire mean, the way he's going." We all jumped. It was Jack, coming up from behind, with others who must have woken up, too.

The horse's red coat was beginning to fleck with sweat. Watching Starfire, I forgot about my job with the day herd. He was a fine-looking animal, with his arching neck and triangular face. Mrs. Hall would have said he had saddlebred blood in him. His slim legs danced against that rope. Running was a horse's best defense against enemies. Starfire could run like this all night—and all the day tomorrow. He could run until he dropped dead; that was a horse's nature.

"A smart horse like that winds up with a bad temper and a tough mouth. It's a crying shame—wish I hadn't introduced 'em." Jack spat, pulled his hat down over his ears, and walked off. Everyone else turned back to the training.

Starfire's mouth was foaming. His eyes rolled but he ran and ran.

"He is too nervous," I whispered to Na-tio. "How can he learn?"

Just then, the buster pulled the lead in, sharp and tight—*snap!* At full speed, the horse was jerked off his front feet. His head popped up and he flipped over—right onto his back!

In that moment, the buster ran in and tied the horse's back leg, pulling it right up toward his nose. I closed my eyes.

The wrangler called out, "You're getting mighty rough with someone else's mount!"

The buster gave a couple of hard slaps on the horse's neck. Starfire's eyes showed white but he didn't even twitch. It was like he was frozen, or dead.

"This devil? We're old friends by now. We're just coming to an understanding—hey, you devil!" *Slap, slap.*

"You let that horse back up," the wrangler's voice shook. "Get off to sleep—we all need some rest."

The buster pushed himself up, took off his heavy gloves and smacked them against his leg.

"I'll get some rest, all right—let ol' devil here think about things for a while." He walked toward camp.

"His name is Starfire," the wrangler called as he followed the buster. "And he oughtta be at field!"

"He's nothin' but a devil to me," the buster said. "I'm gonna roll me a nice cigarette now."

RAQUEL RIVERA

The rest of the hands went back to their bedrolls. They all left the animal on the ground.

"He push too hard," Na-tio said.

"We must help," I replied. Those tight knots were cutting into Starfire. It was bad for his insides to lie down for very long.

"The horse is still frozen, maybe," Na-tio suggested.

"We will untie him," I whispered. "If he's frozen, we won't get kicked!"

"We tie him, but better. Better for horse," Na-tio offered.

It was true. Even if I freed him, and even if Starfire did run—did leave his herd—he'd only be caught on the range, wilder than ever. And I'd be out of work, most likely.

We dismounted and sneaked toward the horse. His belly lifted and fell.

"We tie new ropes, here, and here," Na-tio pursed his lips toward the horse's neck and back leg. Soon we had two lengths tied. Na-tio cut the rope that was holding him bunched tight.

We jumped back.

"Keep the rope!" Na-tio warned.

I grabbed for the end of the neck rope.

Starfire's nostrils fluttered. His belly rose. With a kick and a twist, he was on his feet.

"Hold him!" Na-tio called, while he pulled on the leg rope.

Starfire danced and pulled. He dragged me through his own

manure—I choked and spat. My boots filled.

"Pull!" Na-tio was pulling back on his rope, but Starfire kicked it loose from his hands. The end of the rope flew through the air and then down under Starfire's dancing feet.

Na-tio ran wide and took the neck rope from me. He tugged it in, and then let it out, keeping the horse busy. I rushed around and picked up the leg rope. The buster's rope swung loose, twitching like a fighting snake.

"Hey, you there!" I heard the cry.

"You boys—leave that horse be!"

Na-tio got the neck rope around the stump and he ran to help me tie the leg to a heavy stake in the ground.

"You—get outta there!" It was the boss, running toward us with the owner and Jack. Everyone was following to see what would happen.

Na-tio and I moved away. We had tied Starfire snug—he couldn't buck. But he was straight; he was standing comfortable.

Suddenly, I was dragged off my feet. The boss was holding my shirt with one hand. He held Na-tio in the other. I saw the owner, Mr. Holt. He was frowning.

"What are you boys doing with my horse?" The owner kept his voice low.

I tried to get my breath. The boss was much taller then me; my shirt was being pulled tight across my neck. Na-tio didn't say anything.

"I had him just where I wanted. He was seeing the world in a new light." The buster was smiling. "These boys undone my good work."

The boss snorted. The owner moved past us to Starfire. He put his hand on the horse's side. Starfire stamped, but there wasn't much more he could do.

The boss turned, still holding us, so that Na-tio and I stumbled around with him. We all faced the owner.

"You boys tie up my horse?"

I looked over to Na-tio, but of course he wouldn't speak.

"Just so he was standing. We couldn't leave him the other way," I squeaked out. My throat hurt.

The owner looked at the buster. "Follow me, would you? Tell me about this good work you did." He headed back to camp. The buster followed. The boss let go of my collar and then he followed, too.

I rubbed at my neck. Na-tio straightened his shirt. Starfire was standing.

Jack's hands landed on our shoulders. "I'll bet you two could use some sleep! Shorty and I will take over the rest of your watch." He chuckled, "... and Yipee, clean off the horseshit, wouldya? You stink mighty high for such a little guy."

BAD HUNTING

Na-tio chewed on Shorty's tobacco. Na-tio wouldn't smoke with Anglos, of course. Smoking tobacco was for important moments with his people. But he did like a bit of chewing tobacco.

They had finished a big supper of beans, bacon, and warm biscuits. Yipee was blowing the steam from her coffee. Everyone else was at the other fire, telling stories. Except for Shorty and his friend. They were drinking their coffee here, by Cook's fire.

Then the horse buster came, kicking his spurs. He walked all the way around the fire and sat on the log near Yipee. She moved over to make space; he moved close again.

The horse buster didn't even look at her—he stared at Na-tio on the other side. Na-tio stared back. Yipee was squeezed between the two, but Na-tio wasn't going to move.

"You fittin' in all right, Chief? Like the food?"

Na-tio said nothing.

"Figured you'd do some bronc-busting in your own time—you and your little friend?" He gave Yipee a sharp poke with his elbow.

"Hey," she murmured, rubbing her arm.

Na-tio needed to spit tobacco juice but he held still. The horse buster had a thin white scar along his cheek. It was twitching.

"Hey, Shorty, why they still call you Shorty, now that this rat's come creeping around the outfit?" he called across the fire.

Shorty's friend blew smoke. Shorty pulled at his collar, "Ah, lay off, why don't you? They's just kids. They didn't mean nothing against you."

"Maybe not." The buster hadn't stopped staring at Na-tio. "But I believe they got some harm in 'em." He leaned farther in. Yipee was squeezed tighter.

"'Fore we came out here, there's a man come into Prescott— got robbed of his horses. Almost dead on his feet, he was. The thieves didn't leave him a single mount—not even a packhorse. Vicious, ain't it?"

Shorty was interested. "You mean that bounty hunter? I heard he was near-starved and got the heatstroke bad."

The friend threw his cigarette into the fire. "I heard he had to fight off a pack of wolves."

"I heard it was Indians," the buster said, still watching Na-tio. "But I guess he whupped them cowards easy enough. Got himself a bunch of mangy scalps, too, I bet. What do you think, Chief?"

Na-tio spat out the whole plug; the tobacco was burning his mouth. The horse buster wanted to make him angry. He could feel Yipee's eyes on him, pleading with him not to fight.

He would walk away. He stood up and Yipee followed.

"You boys had some nice enough horses with you when you joined the outfit," the buster called after them. "Where'd you get that Paint, hey, rat?"

"He knows! He knows!" Yipee hadn't trembled like this since the time he had seen her without clothes, washing by the stream. When the buster spoke of the Paint, she'd walked, stiff-legged, to a far-off stand of trees. Now they were hidden from the others.

"So much trouble—too much trouble," she kept saying.

"We go now," Na-tio suggested. "No more trouble."

Yipee stopped trembling. "How do we go? By stealing the owner's horses?" Even among the dark trees, he could see her glare. "And they chase us! And I be outlaw and never work again!" She grabbed a branch and shook it. Her head flopped back as she threw her arms over it. She let out a strange noise. She hung over the branch; her feet trailed in the dust. Her shoulders shook.

He moved to her. Was she crying? He leaned toward her; she was such a little person. He smoothed his hand over her braid, along her back. "Why cry? No one die," he said.

Yipee dropped her head and sighed. But she did stop crying.

RAQUEL RIVERA

After a while she asked, "What do we do?"

Na-tio had been thinking. "You want to stay more—do more roundup?" Yipee nodded.

"Then we stay. We did nothing wrong. That skin-collector hunts bad. He hunt our skin, too, maybe." Na-tio stood up. "He cannot keep his horses because he is a bad hunter and sleeps too hard. I did nothing wrong."

Yipee nodded again, very slow. "Still, maybe I did wrong—a little bit."

"No," Na-tio said. "The skin-collector was wrong. You do roundup if you want."

Yipee ran her hands through her hair. It had grown so much on top that it now fell in her eyes. "But that buster is so angry, he tries to get us killed." She turned to face Na-tio. "They hang horse thieves, did you know? Like from this tree—" she smacked the trunk "—with rope over the branch. And whip our horses so they run—and we drop. And then we turn on the end of the rope, kicking." Her hands flapped like angry birds when she told this story.

"I know what is hanging." Na-tio stood up straight. "But that horse buster, he works bad, too."

Yipee pushed herself off the tree. Na-tio touched her arm so she would look at him, so she could see he spoke true. "We are good."

Then he nudged her toward the light of the fires. "You do roundup."

BRANDING AND CUTTING

"You boys pick out a calf for yourselves, fix up a little brand for it; I don't mind." Mr. Holt, the owner, was looking over the morning's roundup. "I appreciate what you did for Starfire the other night."

I blinked. Na-tio must be right—we were good. Our own calf! Crooked Mah would have been impressed.

The boss was calling everyone back to work. "Day's not over yet!" The branding fires were hot.

Jack roped the first calf around her back legs—pulled her off her feet and dragged her out of the herd. A brander leaned his heavy boot on her and pressed in the Double Y brand. The burning smell rose.

The other ropers could only catch their calves by the head, so they did not drag so well. It was my job, and Na-tio's, to wrestle these calves to the ground for branding—and the knife, if he was a little bull.

RAQUEL RIVERA

The cows and the calves were shouting. The air was hot from the coals. The curses and jokes flew: "Whenever you're finished your tea break, ladies." "Dammit, watch your knife—that's my arm ya near sliced!" Smoke, dirt, and sweat clogged my eyes. The men with the brands ducked in and out, waving their poles. We all kept clear of their red-hot tips.

We worked as fast as we could. Each calf had its own way of fighting. Na-tio's arms were long, so he could get behind and push, while the roper and his horse tugged. I might pull out a leg to make the calf tumble, or pulling an ear might get the head to the ground.

The tallyman's count mixed with all the noise: "Forty-three, male! Forty-four—female! Female! Male! Forty-seven, male!"

We had brought in so many head during roundup today. My arms were heavy. I stopped trying to blink the dust from my eyes. I must keep going until the last calf was branded. Everyone else would; I just had to keep up.

"Fifty-one, fifty-two—male and male!"

The ropers worked fast.

I saw Na-tio's red shirt through rippling air.

"Dammit, Yipee, hold onto that leg—he's gonna kick my brand loose!"

"Excuse; excuse me." The smell of burning hair and skin came up. I must do better. The brander had to jump back twice already when the calf's leg broke away from me.

Na-tio didn't seem tired. It wasn't fair.

The buster came with his penknife for the calf on the ground. There was a yank, a cut, and he was off to the next male. I pushed the calf up and he ran back to the herd, calling for mother. Now all he'd care about was nursing, then eating grass. He'd never want to fight with the bulls. In a few short seasons, he'd be fat for market.

But I must concentrate. Except the buster kept rushing by, which made me remember what he'd done to us this morning—to me and Na-tio.

It was all because the wagon broke. Cook and some others had gone off, looking to cut wood for a new axle. Jack, Shorty, and the wrangler grabbed their bedrolls to catch up on sleep. The rest of us had nothing to do.

"Can't have cowherders at loose ends 'less they're good and tired," Jack liked to say.

A tall hand named Clem was sitting on the ground with his boot off, looking at a spider bite on his heel. The rest of us had gathered around.

"Does that look bigger to you?" he asked.

Everyone agreed that it was swelled pretty bad. "Lucky it ain't snakebite," someone said.

Just then a wolf passed by—not too far away.

"*Hoo*—you bold varmint!" someone cried.

"She smells the calves!"

"I betcha three dollars I rope her!"

"Betcha five you eat my dust!"

The mounted hands kicked their horses and rode toward the wolf. The wolf ran.

The hand named Clem pulled his sock back on.

"They want to chase the wolf?" I asked.

"Why, rat, don't you know? They're gonna rope that wolf—if they can." The buster had been giving Na-tio and me bad looks all morning. The owner had put him on day herd: he'd be stuck at camp while the rest of us got to ride out. But it was his fault for hurting Starfire, not ours. And I wasn't a rat.

"They're just working their ropes—having a little fun at the same time." Clem pulled his boot on, slow and careful.

"These boys prefer stealing for their fun." The buster flicked his cigarette our way.

Na-tio went rigid.

"He's a warrior," I told them. "He's no thief!"

They all laughed.

I felt a jab in my ribs; Na-tio was glaring at me. I glared back—I wasn't going to let them talk bad about him.

The riders were almost on the wolf now. She darted low under the stamping hooves and ran back the way she came. Ropes were thrown and tangled. Cursing, the riders drove her toward the high rocks. The ropes flew and missed again.

"Jack don't have much worry for competition—not with this bunch," Clem said.

"I can think of a better use for my rope." The buster was giving us his bad look again—he wouldn't stop!

Everyone turned. Someone said, "He's been calling you horse-rustlers for a while. Says you left a man without a mount. You got nothing to say about that?"

I glanced at Na-tio but his face had turned to stone.

There was a burst of shouts and cheers by the high rocks. One of the ropes had landed. The wolf was twisting in the dust. The lucky horse and rider backed up hard, pulling the noose tight.

"Yah! You got 'er!"

"You're out five dollars, cowpoke!"

Na-tio looked sad. "Now they bring her in."

The buster's eyes narrowed. "They're not done with 'er yet."

It was true; they let the wolf get on her feet and they all started to ride. At first she kept up, but as they went on, she fell more, until she was bumping and twisting on the end of the rope.

Soon she looked like a ragged scrap of fur, bouncing along the ground.

The cowhands rode in with their wolf.

"That was a morning well spent," declared the one holding the rope.

RAQUEL RIVERA

"The skin might be worth something in town," Clem added.

"You better keep it close by," the buster said. "There's thieves around."

Then Cook was calling. "Git up, you lazy mama's boys! Wagon's fixed—we're rolling!"

Now, at the branding pen, the more I thought about it, the more it seemed like the buster wouldn't stop his bad talk about me and Na-tio until he got us hung.

Maybe I wasn't too weak to wrestle calves; maybe I was just worried.

There he was again! The buster was at Na-tio's calf—I couldn't hear what he said, but Na-tio's face went dark. Then the buster made his cut, but he mustn't have pulled tight enough, because blood spurted high—all over Na-tio. The calf bellowed and the buster hopped up laughing, brushing at the few stray drops that had hit him.

"Maybe a poke with this'll get you working right!" One of the branders was yelling at me and waving his iron in the air.

Oh, no! I'd let the leg slip again!

"'Cause you done that for the last time!" The brander's face was as red as his iron.

"Please excuse, so sorry," I said, over and over.

The boss sent me to mind the fire.

How shameful—I'd failed! I'd let everyone down. Someone could have been hurt. I ran for wood. I pumped the bellows. Those branders would have the highest and hottest fire ever.

Sweat poured down my face. I was so hot, but only from shame. It was true I hadn't been paying good attention, but it was worse: I wasn't strong enough. Everyone else could do the work but not me. I put more wood on the fire.

Then something made me stop and look up. Everything had gone so quiet.

Over there by Na-tio, the brander was standing still, his iron pointing down. What happened?

It was the buster—he was flat on the ground. His hat was rolling toward the herd. I ran over—was he breathing?

"Find Cook! Get Cook over here!" someone shouted.

Na-tio was crouched over the young bull, still holding the back leg just right, up and forward, as if the buster was going to get up and start cutting again.

He was holding that calf's leg like a slingshot.

"It slipped," he said.

"Coming through—get out of the way—bosses coming through!" I was pushed aside and could only see tall, sweat-soaked backs.

"Get him to the wagon—get him out of the sun!"

"He'll be all right!"

"His head is harder 'n any hoof I ever met."

RAQUEL RIVERA

"That's as may be but I couldn't see 'im breathing."

The boss called out, "Simmer down! Mr. Holt says the man's gotta wake up, then we'll know—so get back to work!" As the hands moved away, he flapped his arms and made pushing motions, like we were a bunch of chickens.

"We'll keep him in our prayers but we got to finish the day out." He turned to Clem. "You'll take over cutting."

Clem crossed his long arms and shook his head. "I'll cut, but not on his calves."

Everyone looked at Na-tio. He released the young bull, which scrambled back to the herd. No one else moved.

Then the noise started again:

"What happened, anyway?

"What's he got to say for himself?"

"Dirty Indian, horse thief, horsethief."

"Horsethiefhorsethiefhorsethief."

I covered my ears and tried to send Na-tio a message. But to say what? If only I knew—if only he would look at me!

But Na-tio only watched the boss, even with all those eyes on him. He looked calm; his face had gone light again.

He pulled off the handkerchief that was tied around his head, and wiped the blood and dirt from his cheeks. He looked up at the sky, like when it was only the two of us.

"Na-tio," I prayed. "Na-tio ..."

"I made a mistake," he told the sky.

And then he bowed his head with his kerchief held in both hands. We had seen Jack, Shorty, and the rest of them do this on a Sunday.

Everyone was quiet. The boss stood there.

A hard slap on my shoulder made me jump. "Mistakes happen, hey, Yipee?" It was Jack. I nodded and nodded. After all, I'd let many legs fly this afternoon. Everyone knew that.

"I don't mind cutting if everyone else is too scared." Jack said. "I can keep track of my own head, even if other folks can't."

The boss clapped his hands together "All right, finish the herd—never mind the chattering, neither—y'all keep your minds and your mouths on your work!"

CHAPTER

24

VIGIL

Cook was too busy tending to the buster, so the wrangler cooked supper that night. Jack often said a cowherder didn't know a good chuck wagon until he'd ridden behind a bad one. As I spooned up boiled bacon and porridge, I understood his meaning.

Na-tio wouldn't touch the food. That was all right for him, but I needed my strength; I didn't want to fail at branding time tomorrow.

"How's he doing, Mr. Bart?" Everyone turned to the boss, who was coming up to the fire. His mustaches seemed to droop more than usual. Everyone was sober tonight, and it wasn't just because of the wrangler's supper. Our minds were on the buster, lying in Cook's wagon.

The boss sat down and about a dozen tin plates were offered.

"You want some grub, boss?"

"I couldn't hardly eat mine."

"Mr. Bart'll take mine; it ain't even been touched."

The boss reached for a plate and stabbed his pocket-knife into the meat. He examined it, eyes bugging. "Here now, what part of what animal might I be fixing to eat?"

He was told that the wrangler had boiled the bacon for a change of pace.

The boss was looking so close at the meat, his eyes crossed. "That's fine. Why is it green?"

It was explained that the wrangler seasoned his boil-water with some kind of plant. "It don't taste of much, but it sure got color." Clem was picking his teeth with a stick.

The boss put the plate on the ground. "I'll just have coffee."

A cup was offered. He sipped, winced, and took out his flask. He poured a measure into his coffee. "Cook'll be on for breakfast—"

Everyone went still. Did this mean the buster was all right, or beyond fixing?

"It don't mean nothing." The boss slumped down so his boots almost touched the fire. "Only there isn't much Cook can do. The buster'll get better himself—or he'll decide to leave all his troubles behind."

Murmurs began to ripple among the hands. They'd been sneaking looks at Na-tio all evening; now the looks were bolder and mean. There was a bad feeling in the air.

But nobody had much liked the buster when he was well—had they forgotten? Besides, it was an accident, wasn't it?

RAQUEL RIVERA

None of these men knew Na-tio like I did. Na-tio wouldn't bother anybody that didn't bother him first. They hadn't seen him out on the range, rescuing a calf from a stream. Or feeding a horse his own portion of sugar. I knew Na-tio; he was smart and brave and the best friend anyone could ever ask for.

I also knew Na-tio wasn't clumsy or weak, like me. But sometimes accidents happened.

The boss didn't seem to notice the bad feeling. He mumbled about seeing the owner and Cook, and moved off.

The hands exchanged glances. They moved closer. One of the bigger men picked up a coil of rope. Na-tio stood up.

"You're not going anywhere." The man with the rope slapped it against his thigh. I looked around. Eyes had gone squinty, mouths hard and ugly.

We'd all been riding together, friendly-like, up until now. Some of these men had told funny jokes.

But now they were like a wall. That wall crowded around Na-tio.

"I made a mistake." That was all Na-tio would say when the boss and the owner had quizzed him about the accident. "I made a mistake," Na-tio repeated now, looking steady at the hand with the rope.

I broke through the wall to stand by Na-tio. "Accidents happen …" I stopped. My eyes flicked from one face to another.

"The buster wasn't so keen on you, either," someone snarled.

"There's nothing wrong with us," I cried. "It's not our fault he hated us!" But the wall closed in.

Someone grabbed my hands and feet and I was twisting in the air. Where were they taking us?

"Na-tio!" I screamed, but he didn't make a sound. He wouldn't give them the satisfaction of hearing him shout.

"*Ow*—damnation—the heathen bites!" I heard a soft thud and a groan.

I couldn't see what they were doing to Na-tio. We were moving so fast—and it was dark. Where were they taking us?

"Get horses," someone commanded, and my arms were dropped. My head crashed to the ground and things got fuzzy as I bumped along, dragged by my legs. Why did they want horses? It was hard to think, my head bumping like that, but then I remembered about hanging. They wanted to put us on horses, with nooses around our necks!

I kicked, hit a soft spot, and there was cursing as my legs fell to the ground. I turned over and scrambled to my feet, but was soon trapped again. At least I was standing.

Na-tio was there, breathing hard, trapped between two others. Blood ran from his mouth. His face was twisted—his nostrils were flaring. He looked a bit like Starfire, tied to a trunk. If Na-tio was afraid, things must be very bad for us. My legs would've crumpled under me if I wasn't being held so tight.

RAQUEL RIVERA

And then someone spoke in the dark.

"It's a real shame. I'm sorry for the buster." The voice sounded familiar.

I blinked; they'd brought us to the corral. But new men blocked the way. It was Jack. And there was Shorty, and the wrangler, too. They blocked the way to the corral—to the horses.

They seemed to be in deep conversation with one another. They didn't seem to notice me and Na-tio. They didn't greet the others.

Jack was holding Cook's rifle. He pointed the barrel to the ground before him and looked down it, like he was considering to buy it.

It was the rifle that stopped the others. "We'll be getting a couple of horses for these varmints—we're gonna string them up, on account of ol' buster." The hand with the rope cleared his throat. "We aim to pass now ..."

Nobody moved out of their way. The wrangler was talking to Jack.

"Poor buster. He does have a knack for stirring trouble, don't he? I didn't like his way with the horses."

"Kinda like your way with a side of bacon," Shorty joked. The wrangler shook his head and laughed.

Jack cocked the rifle and lifted it to his sight. He gave it a casual swing across the group before him. Everyone stepped back. "Cook claims he caught a buck at fifty paces with this thing. I can't feature it." He rested the firearm across his front and went back to the conversation.

"Lord knows, we've all made mistakes. I'm sure the buster had his reasons for disliking those two boys—though they never did me a hair's harm."

Shorty and the wrangler agreed that the boys had been no trouble—none at all—since roundup began.

The grip on me loosened. Na-tio was allowed to reach to his face to wipe away blood.

Shorty took off his hat and studied the inside. "The buster's always got his own reasons for doing things."

Jack seemed suddenly to notice the group before him. "Hey, Clem, remember when the buster tricked you out of that silver medallion your pa left you?" Jack chuckled. "Yeah, he's a smart one, the buster."

The wrangler nodded. "Smart, yes. Wouldn't want to rely on 'im, though. Zebediah, was you the one he left alone with that mad steer, last roundup?"

Na-tio and I were released. The big hand looked at his rope, like he was surprised to see it there. He slung it over his shoulder.

Jack moved in, cutting me and Na-tio from the herd—suddenly we were standing with him, Shorty, and the wrangler. It was as if the whole outfit just happened to be jawing, out here by the wrangler's patch.

RAQUEL RIVERA

"It seems like the Lord loves an imperfect man. I know on that count we all measure up. I sure hope the buster gets better. Meantime, the rest of us, we got to pull together—roundup ain't half finished."

There were shuffles and shrugs among the group.

"If the little 'un sticks to stoking fire at branding time, I guess that's all right," someone said.

"And no more wrestling for the Injun. Make 'im cut calves— put his own head at risk."

Na-tio nodded. "I made a mistake," he admitted.

"Me too—I made many mistakes," I added.

Jack shouldered the rifle. "Cook's a better shot than me. At fifty paces, dunno as I could hit the side of a hill with this old piece."

Then Shorty suggested, even though it wasn't Sunday, we all should pray for the buster to get well, and also for smooth rides and sunny days to finish roundup.

CHAPTER

๑ 25 ๑

CATTLE TRAIL

For Na-tio, a season on the ranch passed slower than anywhere else. It was like that Clem's pocket watch—tick, tick, tick: drive cows, brand them, send them back on the range, and do it again.

The horse buster had woken up. He didn't know anybody and had trouble walking at first. Then he stayed with the day herd, "until he's feeling more himself," the owner had said.

But that didn't happen. The buster couldn't ride fast anymore; he would get dizzy and drop the reins. Also, sometimes he forgot what he wanted to say, and spit would drip from his mouth instead. But he wasn't mean anymore. He had stopped bothering Yipee and making Na-tio angry. It seemed like he didn't remember them. When the others were told to come back for fall roundup, the owner kept the buster at the ranch.

The owner had asked Na-tio and Yipee to stay, too. Na-tio would prefer to camp in the hills but Yipee wanted to work. Maybe she would come away soon.

One day, the horse buster was out fixing fences when the horse came back alone. It didn't take long to find his body.

They said it was a bruise inside his head. They said it was a blessing. They buried him in the ground. They said his soul was at rest now. Na-tio thought that was all fine. But the important thing was the buster would not bother anyone—horses or people—anymore.

Then summer was over. The others returned and it was roundup—again. And still, Yipee was not tired of it!

Now they were taking the animals away. The owner was selling his cattle for others to eat. It began to seem that Yipee would never want to leave.

Every morning they were up before light and moving along the trail. They moved fast to tire out the animals so they would not stampede.

Na-tio and Yipee rode at the back, in the dust kicked up by the herd.

"We used to travel where we pleased," Na-tio reminded her. Yipee laughed.

Na-tio could leave without her. He could travel alone. Or he could look for Father's people. But every time he had this idea, the pain pierced behind his eyes and he had to blink.

Thinking about living the old way, among his people, reminded him of Mother—and everyone who was gone. How could

Na-tio be always remembering, always in pain? He didn't want to return, but he didn't like being here, either.

At least here was Yipee. Brave little Yipee.

He chased after a cranky old cow and drove her forward. Another rider appeared in the dust; it was Jack, signaling that Na-tio should ride to the front of the herd. Na-tio looked for Yipee through the dust and the animals, but he couldn't find her. Jack gestured again that Na-tio should move up.

Na-tio gave the horse his heels and rode forward. Today he had a gelding with a hard mouth. Na-tio urged him to a gallop, so they were both warm by the time they reached the front.

Up here, everyone had stopped. The cattle were getting restless. Na-tio pulled down his kerchief and sucked in the clear air. He rode up to the boss's group.

Then Na-tio saw why they all looked so worried.

There were warriors on horseback, far away, by that tree. They wanted some animals for their families, maybe. They were only three but they could start a stampede, easy. The people would then help themselves, and the boss and hands would be looking for the rest of their cattle for many days.

"What do you guess they want, Chief?" the boss asked. Na-tio heard the thudding of hooves. It was Yipee riding up.

The boss nodded at Yipee and Na-tio. "You boys are going to help me parlay with those scroungers over there." He turned

RAQUEL RIVERA

to the others. "I'll see if we can get 'em off our backs with a head or two."

Yipee squinted into the distance, like she could hardly see the people out there on the horizon. The others settled back in their saddles. Clem pulled out a pouch and rolled a cigarette with a small square of newspaper. The boss turned his horse and held out his hand.

"Toss me that pouch—it may come in handy with the savages."

"This is supposed to last me to Mission," Clem protested.

"Ain't that sad." The boss wiggled his fingers, waiting. Clem gave the tobacco and jammed his hat down over his ears, grumbling. The boss urged his horse forward; Na-tio and Yipee followed.

The three warriors waited under the shade of a cottonwood. They rode little wild horses.

Na-tio saw that the tallest warrior carried two rifles, along with the bow on his back. His legs were bare, even in this cold air. Na-tio's legs itched in their trousers. He pulled at the dusty kerchief hanging around his neck.

They rode in closer. Na-tio stared at the warrior; his belly loosened. He could feel Yipee was staring, too; her mouth dropped as she looked from the warrior to him and back. Even the boss saw it.

Everyone always said that Na-tio looked very much like Uncle.

Uncle hid his surprise through half-dropped eyelids. Na-tio

did not know the other warriors. Uncle's horse came forward into the sunlight.

"It is no trick of light," Uncle said. "You are my sister's son."

"It is me." Na-tio tried to keep his voice steady. The other warriors remained in the shade.

The boss urged his horse forward and interrupted in English, "Looks like we got ourselves a family reunion!" He tried to make it a joke but his eyes were flicking—from the warriors to Na-tio.

Na-tio's face felt frozen. This was a shock: Uncle. The last time he saw Uncle was at the cabin with those fluttering curtains. Na-tio heard the laughter as if he was there again.

It was the baby that laughed. In the cabin, the baby was laughing at the curtains. Now the sound came back—laughing at him.

That boss was squinting at him, wondering which way Na-tio would go. And Uncle—was Uncle ashamed for Na-tio, all trussed up in trousers?

And who were these other warriors—where was the chief? Where was Father?

A cool wind blew, stirring the tree. Yipee's horse jumped at a twitching shadow.

Na-tio felt a chill. He had disobeyed; he had run. He had dishonored himself and his elders.

"There, there, settle now, you foolish thing," Yipee was murmuring to the crazy horse she'd picked out this morning.

Well, Na-tio wouldn't run away, not this time.

He felt his face thaw as he told Yipee, "This is my uncle." Na-tio couldn't help it if Uncle thought he was a disgrace.

Yipee smiled, but Uncle gave her such a scowl that her mouth dropped again.

"You ride with strangers." Uncle was angry. "You run from your family to ride with–" he looked hard at the boss with his stringy mustaches, and then back at Yipee, who suddenly seemed very small in her saddle, "–with these pitiful creatures," Uncle finished.

"You know about Mother?" Na-tio asked. His voice broke just to say it; he couldn't help it. His nose stung and he blinked.

Please let Uncle know. He didn't think he could tell what happened to Mother, not out loud.

Uncle slumped a little. "Your father has gone to war over this. He went south and joined those who fight." He looked over at Yipee and the boss, speaking louder, this time in English, "Soldiers, miners, ranchers–he is against them all until they go back where they came from."

Then he said to Na-tio, "You are his second family that has been murdered. Now he devotes himself to war."

"But you do not fight with him," Na-tio said.

"I do not fight for now," Uncle confirmed.

"I do not fight, either," Na-tio asserted.

Uncle looked down. "Your father will be happy to know that you are alive. He would want you with him. If he seemed harsh, it was to make you stronger."

Na-tio would never be strong like Father. After all, he didn't go to war after the soldiers killed everyone. He had meant to, truly, but Yipee had delayed him. Now he found he didn't have the spirit for it.

"We have to be strong, Nephew, now more than ever."

Na-tio blinked hard. Uncle wasn't at war. So then there were other ways to be strong. It was good to talk with Uncle again. Was it true that Father wanted him? He waited for the headache to come.

The boss interrupted. "Tell him he can have a steer for his squaw, so we may take safe passage through his land."

"You join me," Uncle suggested to Na-tio. "You and I, we will finish your learning together. You will be a great warrior, like your father."

"All right, two steer," the boss spoke louder. "Two fat steer, but he guarantees that none of his people will be back for more."

The boss turned to Yipee for help. Her eyes bulged, then she raised her hands and shrugged. Na-tio smiled at this. She was a small person, but she always sat well and straight.

"I learn now," Na-tio explained to Uncle. "For now, I go this way."

"This makes me sad," Uncle said. "Your father will be sad."

Na-tio felt a little rip inside. But not so strong as when he lost Mother, because now he knew something: Father and Uncle were always in him. He wanted Yipee by his side.

"I will decide," Na-tio told Uncle as gently as he could.

Uncle's mouth went thin, but he nodded and turned his horse back to the waiting warriors. "You must look for me if ever you want. Your father, too—he will always want you to look for him."

"Yes, Uncle," Na-tio whispered. He closed his eyes, ready for the pain—but his head remained clear and easy. Maybe he would meet Father again.

"Is it agreed, then?" the boss asked. All the warriors gazed at him with stone faces.

"My uncle says he must have many animals, because he is responsible for too many people." Na-tio's arm reached out and spanned the lands to the north and the west. "Seven animals he wants, and his people will not bother you for more."

Uncle heard this and laughed, his mouth wide like a wound.

FAMILY

"Dammit to the devil ..." The boss's cursing was slowing down. He had been listing all the bad luck things on this drive, starting with the loss of seven head to Na-tio's uncle. Then he cursed Clem, who had disappeared with a good horse during a drinking spree. "He turns up, I'll stuff 'im with his own boots," the boss had promised.

The rest of the hands had mumbled that it wasn't decent of Clem to sneak liquor and not share. Hands weren't allowed to drink on the trail, so they were all feeling parched by this time.

And now this. Even Jack looked upset. We had barely got the herd started this morning when a steer fell, screaming. Its leg was snapped in a wagon wheel hidden in the grass. Cook ran to the sound, cocking his rifle. He pressed behind the animal's ear and fired. There was quiet.

But the sounds and smells had upset the herd, and the boss started shouting to move on quick.

"No one leaves a wagon wheel out here," Jack was warning over the rumble of the herd. "There's a lame wagon not far. Maybe folks needing help—"

"That's as never mind to me." The boss broke off to curse some more. "This lot's getting to Mission—before I lose any more to the infernal luck of this run!" He waved his hat, giving the signal to move. Over his shoulder, he ordered Na-tio and me to stay and butcher the steer with Cook.

Later, Na-tio found the rest of the wagon.

Smoke rose off its burnt cover, the round frame poking through like a skeleton. Cook, Na-tio, and I were messy with the blood of the steer. We looked as if we had attacked this settler wagon ourselves.

While Na-tio searched the grass in widening circles, I climbed the wagon to see inside.

It was empty; my breath came out in a low hiss. I was happy not to see people ripped apart, like the ones I had found at the cabin.

The back end of the wagon was black with smoke. Whatever these settlers had carried with them—cooking pots, farming tools, firearms, food, seed—someone else had it now.

Since seeing the wagon, Cook hadn't moved. "Nope," he whispered. His head started turning from side to side like a reluctant calf. "I'm done with this," he said, as if we had been talking all along.

I turned and jumped to the ground. Cook stared at the wagon

like he was seeing ghosts. Maybe he had his own memories, like my cabin and Na-tio's cave. I looked for Na-tio. He was making broad sweeps at the grass. Cook and I watched him stop. He raised his arm high, still looking down. He had found something.

"Nope," Cook said again, very quiet. Then, like a crazy person, he shouted at Na-tio's waving arm: "No!"

He turned away, his bloody apron flapping, "Let me get to Mission in one piece ..." he was begging the sky. For such a big man, Cook moved fast.

I called after him but he kept going. "Catch up if you want," he shouted. "I got a chuck wagon to drive—"

Na-tio was watching us, eyes squinting against the sun. I ran to him.

He stood inside a burned circle in the grass. The tangled bodies were blackened like people-shaped coal. They must have been tied together when they were set alight. They must have died writhing like snakes, to be all twisted around each other like that.

There was a grown man, slender boys, and a woman whose skirts must have burned high around them all. Poor family.

I remembered Na-tio running among his own family as they lay dead on the ground. So this was fair, maybe. Was Na-tio happy to see this?

But he only looked very, very tired. "This never ends, I think." He was looking through me, as if there was someone else behind with an answer. We waited for it together.

I wanted to reach out and smooth those hard lines around his mouth, his eyes. The smell of burned flesh was sick-making.

But these bodies did not haunt me like the ghosts at the cave. They didn't scare me like at the cabin. They did not make me too sad, like Crooked Mah. I must be getting used to this Gold Mountain.

First I thought to bury their bones; it was the only thing I could do for them. But we had no pick or shovel.

"The land will take them." Na-tio whispered, as if hearing my thoughts.

"Maybe we say something over them," I suggested, since foreigners did this for their dead. Na-tio looked at me, waiting.

"All right." I coughed. "This family was strong and brave ..." Na-tio's stone-face was making me nervous, so I turned to the twisted knot on the ground. "We know this because they were searching ... with ideas ..." I didn't have English words to say what I wanted. I meant that this family followed their spirit, no matter it wasn't safe to do. And they died following their idea. And maybe this was the best anyone could hope for ... maybe. That was what I wanted to say. "Now, you." I told Na-tio.

He gazed down at the family and then lifted his face to the distance. He let out a long, low sound that grew higher and made my insides turn with sadness. He sang some words I didn't know, until his voice broke and he stopped.

His breathing was harsh and ragged so I reached for him. "These now join the others I carry." He blinked at me, his eyes wet. "They join Mother, and Father's first family, and also a baby I did not know. I can carry these, too," he nodded at the figures on the ground.

I gripped Na-tio's big hand as strong as I could. I tried to help him carry all his people. When he squeezed back, it felt like he was helping to carry mine. We returned to the horses, walking like this.

We camped by the wagon for the night. We would catch up to the others tomorrow.

"Yipee." The campfire was making shadows in Na-tio's face. I jumped because it was the first time he ever said my name. He smiled at me, laughing a little bit.

"I never heard my name in your mouth," I defended myself.

"We don't speak names like you," he agreed. "Only for very important things." His face went serious and I shivered. "You are cold." He put his blanket over me. I was not cold but did not say so. I liked how his hands felt, smoothing the blanket around my shoulders, over my arms.

I reached for his hand because I wanted to feel it again, like before. It was warm, rough, and dry.

"I must speak something and hope you will listen." The same way his blanket was around me, so were his eyes. They were finding me. This is what was making me shiver. He was making me nervous. He seemed different, except, as I saw his eyes, I knew it was me who hadn't seen him before.

I kept my ears open. I kept watching this new-old Na-tio.

"When we first met on the land, I was ..." He straightened up "... I wanted to be a grown warrior when I was not." He took a deep breath and huddled back close to me. He glared at the fire. I held myself very still so he wouldn't let go of my hand.

"There is a good way to hunt. And I ..." he sighed, "... I killed, not like a warrior but like a trapped weakling–" his words came fast and not all in English. I pressed closer. I wanted to share the blanket he had given, reaching around him as far as I could. But Na-tio had asked me to listen.

He spoke of his father and a raid. Or maybe it was his uncle. "Your uncle under the trees?" I wanted to ask, but I had promised to listen. He spoke of a baby. He said he killed a baby because there was no good way. It didn't make sense, so maybe I heard wrong. There was so much killing and hurt on this Gold Mountain.

"I thought Father made this happen to me." He looked fierce, like I was trying to say something different. But I held his eyes. I pretended he was looking at his troubles, not at me. Then I was brave enough to listen.

"So it was difficult to think of my father. More difficult even than carrying the burned ones who are not my people!" His hand flew to the darkness beyond, where the family lay in the grass. His eyes flickered with firelight when he turned to me. "It is because of the baby that I promised to carry the burned ones over there. Because of my mistake, I now carry Anglos, too." Then his voice went almost too low to hear. "Father did not make me this way."

Then he dropped my hand. The cold night air came between us. "I chose." His mouth made its thin line. "I honor my father," he told the dying fire. "But I am not the warrior he is."

Then he settled back down and saw me again. I stirred the flames before putting on the last of our wood. He held out his arm and I returned to his side.

"You are a good warrior, Na-tio." I reminded him how he saved me many times, from the wolf, from the skin-collector, how he taught me to hunt, and how brave he was about the buster, when everyone wanted us hung dead.

He shrugged. "This is not what I started to tell you." His low, wide voice rolled through me, and I couldn't help opening the blanket to bring it around him, too. "Yipee. I wanted to tell you: *this* is what I like most. Camping, with you."

Then he ran his fingers along my cheek. I stopped breathing. "So round." His eyes were wet again. "I always like to see your round face. Since the very first time."

I leaned forward and didn't stop, until my mouth had made his soft and part of me.

CHAPTER

⇒ 27 ⇐

CHILD

Yipee made noises when she slept. Na-tio put his head closer so he could feel her breathing. If only she would choose him and not the cattle-trail, they could travel like this always. He curled around her soft form, her tiny bones. She had kissed him in the night. She had shown him how it was between warriors and wives—they had shown each other. He breathed in the sweet, salty smell behind her ear.

But then the sounds returned, the snapping and snarling that had woken him.

A pack—coyotes, likely—must have found the burned family. They were not too near but the horses were nervous, so Na-tio slipped from the blankets to shorten their leads. They must not run away. He rubbed their noses because he didn't have any sugar to give them.

Na-tio would build the fire high to keep the pack from this place. He moved to the wrecked wagon and pulled off another plank. They had been feeding the fire all night with the floorboards, pried up with a knife. Since there was no axe, Na-tio and Yipee had been placing each long plank over the fire, breaking it into smaller parts as it burned through.

Yipee. Thinking about Yipee made him float like there was a soft cloud between Na-tio and the ground—between his hand and the plank as he stirred up the coals. It made him strong; he could do anything and this cloud would protect him. Just like when he was holding Yipee, kissing. Only that was better, because then she was in the cloud, too. Strong and soft, everything was the good way with Yipee.

Na-tio looked over to the blankets, rising and falling with her breathing. He thought to climb in again—take her kisses again.

But first the fire must be higher. The pack must not pass through the cloud.

Prying up another plank, Na-tio thought of Yipee telling him the story of the wolf. It was true, after all: he had been like a warrior—brave, strong, fast. Na-tio had outsmarted the wolf with his knife. It was a good moment. But he knew something else: back then, Na-tio was thinking always of his father ... how others might see him. He had been thinking of the outside when the inside was the important thing: how Na-tio saw himself.

Now this next plank was stuck. Na-tio twisted the wood around. He braced himself against the wagon and pulled up—*snap, creak!*

RAQUEL RIVERA

Traveling with Yipee, Na-tio saw that he was warrior and novice both.

Another twist and the plank would be free. Soon Na-tio would be under the blankets.

Yipee would be warm and damp. Her skin came to him as if his face was against her neck already—*crack!* Finally the plank was free. It thumped to the ground below. Na-tio hopped down.

But wait, what was here, under the wagon? The ground had been dug here, with a real shovel. Lumps of earth and grass were hiding something—

"Mmm. What did you find?" Yipee was awake, rubbing her porcupine hair and yawning.

"A box ... a crate." There was a lid. Through the slats, Na-tio could see something had been hidden from the attackers.

He felt Yipee behind him, leaning in under the wagon. He brushed the last grasses off the top and lifted. It was a child. Her long braids, stuck between the slats, were pulled up with the lid.

"*Ai-yo,*" Yipee breathed. She took the lid from Na-tio. He slipped his hand inside the woolen coat that was bundled around the little form. The crate was almost too small but the child had curled tight.

"She is warm," Na-tio announced, gathering the woolen bundle in both arms.

"Her family must have hoped to return for her."

Na-tio scooped up the bundle. It was surprising how light the child was. She must have quail-bones, full of air. She opened her eyes to him. Quiet, blinking. They were the color of clouds on a stormy day. Her mouth opened but no sound came out.

"She needs water ..." Na-tio brought her by the fire. She was too weak to walk on her own. She seemed awake but still in a dream. Her eyes never left Na-tio.

Then Yipee was there, tipping the canteen for the child. "She doesn't want to drink."

Na-tio asked Yipee to dip his kerchief in the water. He took the cloth and wet those cracked lips, squeezing a few drops onto her tongue. The storm-eyes churned. Na-tio thought he saw little flashes of lightning.

"She will take water now," he urged, so Yipee offered again. This time the child drank. "Not too much at first," he cautioned, taking the canteen as the child sat up in his arms. She was so small. A spray of tiny spots ran across her face, as if someone had flicked a brush of war paint. He touched one to see if it would come off, and she held his finger. The small hand held him fast.

Then Yipee was offering meat; soft liver from the parts that Cook had left behind in his rush. Liver meat was very good. It would make the child strong.

"I have no salt to make it tasty," Yipee murmured, but the child snatched with both hands, tearing at it, as blood oozed from

RAQUEL RIVERA

the barely cooked flesh. "I should have left it on the fire longer."

But Na-tio laughed out loud. "This is good, like this. I thought to call her Bird for her light bones and sky-pale eyes. Now I think we call her Wolf."

Then the child stopped eating. She glanced at Yipee before glaring up at Na-tio. "My name's Mary, not Wolf." Na-tio felt his face split into a grin. He looked at Yipee. This child was very good!

"Please to meet you, Mary." Yipee blinked until her eyes stopped popping from her head. "You want more to eat?" Mary nodded but, when Na-tio tried to put her down, she clung tight.

So they ate together like this, munching Yipee's bits of roasted liver, hot from the coals, and taking sips of water. In the distance, Na-tio heard the pack going quiet. It was time for them to rest; the day had dawned. Na-tio wondered if Mary knew what had happened to her family. She must have heard things from her hole in the ground.

"We catch up to the others now." Yipee was packing up the bedrolls. "We can bring Mary to Mission. They will look after her there."

MISSION

Mission was the first stop on the boss's cattle run. The town grew up in the valley as mining companies were digging gold out of the hills. Everyone wanted beef to eat. Several head were sold here, while the rest were put to pasture to fatten up, before we moved on.

This gave me a few days in Mission to find Mary a home. Shorty said there were nuns further along the trail who might take her in. But the boss said I should leave her in Mission. The trail was no place for Mary, he said.

Up and down the main road I walked. The saloon, with its hotel above, was the biggest, grandest building on the row. But no matter how rich the saloonkeeper, a hotel was no place to raise a child.

Of course, the jail wasn't any good, either. But as I passed the big star painted on the front door, I thought how a sheriff would make a fine guardian. Mary would be safe with a lawman, after all. I pushed on that big star, creaking the door open. The sheriff might have a pretty wife who would like a child of her own.

"Good day," I called. The place seemed empty. There was a desk and some straight chairs. There was a tall cabinet with a big lock. "Good day?"

"Yipee!"

I jumped, turned, and saw the bars of the jail cell right behind me—someone was locked in there. I backed up, knocking against the desk. "Yipee, it's me, Clem."

"What?" It was Clem, his hands around the bars now, his face pressed up so I could see him. "Why?" I managed. He had a black eye and a big cut across the top of his nose, which was now squashed to one side. "What happened, Clem?"

"Yipee, you got to tell the boss I didn't mean nothin'!" He smelled sour, like old fear and too much drink. "Tell him I'm real sorry; the boss knows how I get when I drink spirits—I can't help myself."

"The boss is mad at you. You took his horse." I said.

"I don't make a mistake twice—you tell 'im, Yipee—he knows that." Clem hung his head until I thought it would touch his knees. "If the boss'll vouch for me with the sheriff, he'll get my best work the whole rest of the run, without pay. Tell 'im that, would ya?"

"I'll tell him," I promised. "Does your face hurt much?"

Clem slumped back onto the little cot, making it bang against the wall. "Only when I breathe." He snorted at his joke, and then groaned and held his nose.

"Did you meet the sheriff?" I hadn't forgotten my reason for being here. "Is he good?"

"He's got a good left jab, if that's what you mean." Clem stretched out, swearing that if he ever took another drop, he'd cut off his trigger-finger.

I had to keep looking for Mary's new home.

"Goodbye, Clem. I will tell the boss," I assured him. "First thing I see him."

I passed the sawmill, then the smithy. It was too bad Mary was not a little boy. In a few years, a little boy would make a good blacksmith's apprentice. The problem was that Mary was still young to be any use.

But this didn't matter to Na-tio. He carried her all the time, even though she was big enough to walk by herself. But she would only walk if Na-tio held her hand. If he let go for any reason, she would scream. Na-tio didn't even mind. He never smiled so much since he found Mary in the ground.

I had helped tie her to his back when we rode to Mission. We used a blanket and the long straps of a saddle bag, crossing them around the front, then tying them under Mary's legs.

"You look like a woman," I told him, but Na-tio didn't seem to hear. Mary was tickling his ear with a bit of grass.

RAQUEL RIVERA

She did look sweet, all snuggled up against him like a frog on a tree trunk. And she was quiet and good all the way to Mission, which was some hard riding. And at night, camping with the others on the meadow outside town, all the hands enjoyed her squeaky little voice. "You're fat!" she told Cook when he gave her a special dish of stew and porridge.

"Eat up," Cook replied, "so you can be fat like me." Everyone laughed as she bent over the plate to scoop in porridge faster.

Jack whittled her an alligator from a branch and told stories of his days in Florida—how those bumpy, lizard-creatures would dart from the swamps, dragging horses and riders back in with them. With big eyes, Mary listened, even letting go of Na-tio to stroke Jack's mustaches. "My daddy has mustaches," she told him. Jack choked up and couldn't finish his story. No one had the heart to say about her daddy. Anyhow, from her hiding place in the box, she must have heard everything.

The trail was no place for a little girl—everyone agreed on that. But now, in Mission, it seemed there weren't any good places for a little girl, either. I should have remembered; this was something Crooked Mah and I had known when I was growing up.

If only Mary was bigger. She was too short to carry water; any pail would drag on the ground. She was still too little to drive a team. Maybe she could collect eggs. Maybe a farmer's wife would take her. Then, up the bare slope, I saw just what I was looking for: inside the fenced-in graveyard, among tilting crosses and red earth, there was a woman.

Her skirt puffing high, she was bent over a garden plot that surrounded the biggest and fanciest cross in the yard. I ran up the hill.

She shielded her eyes and watched me coming. We met outside the little gate and she tied it shut with some wire. I spoke to her as well as I knew how. This was the most ladylike lady I'd ever met. Not for her fine clothes and the bonnet that protected her pale face. It was her manners. She greeted me—a dark, dusty cowherder—as if I was a gentleman.

As I explained about Mary, I looked up from my boots to peek at her thin, refined face. She would be a good mistress; her eyes were kind and gentle when she heard the story.

She agreed to take Mary, just like that. Her husband was a preacher, she explained, and they both tried to do what was right. They were new in town, and her husband, Mr. Willet, was trying to start up a regular prayer meeting for town folk, miners, and farmers in the county. "There are so many souls needing guidance," she explained. "Mr. Willet aims to help. I would do my best to follow his example with your little Mary ..." her voice wobbled as she glanced at the big cross in the graveyard, then back to me. "I'm sure it is God's will."

She pointed out her house, a clapboard on the far side of

the graveyard. It even had a porch with a big stack of firewood. I could see it was a good home for a little girl, with educated, genteel people. There must be cushions and rugs and books inside. Mrs. Willet had long, delicate fingers that looked as if they did needlework and played piano. Mary was lucky; I arranged to bring her at suppertime. This gave me enough time to fix her up.

"It is nice—see?" I splashed warm water from the canvas tub onto my own face and made a big smile for Mary. The hotel room was plain and could be rented by the hour, for cowhands' needs. For an extra charge, the serving girl had brought in the tub and pails of hot water. A sliver of hard brown soap lay on the towel she had left. Na-tio was sitting in the only chair, leaning it on its back legs against the wall. He held Mary's dress in his lap. Her bloomers still flapped around her knees, and she was jumping from one corner to the other to escape the bath.

I glared at Na-tio—he should help; Mary listened to him— but he only shrugged. He and Mary agreed that a bath was unnecessary. They didn't understand that Mr. and Mrs. Willet were refined people. Mary's knees, knuckles, and fingernails were dark with dirt—as if she hadn't washed at all along the wagon trail. Her time in the ground hadn't helped, either.

"You go in the bath!" she cried at me, cramming herself into the corner by the coat stand.

Na-tio grinned at this. "Good idea." He put his hands behind his head. "You like baths. We will watch." His smile made me think of the two of us, under blankets by the fire. I wished it was just the two of us now.

But even though Na-tio made me fuzzy-headed, he gave me a new plan.

"If I get in, you must come, too," I told Mary with a stern face. Crooked Mah would never stand for back-talk. When I was little, he always made me do what he wanted.

Mary looked over to Na-tio, who was busy watching me undress. Her gray eyes darted between me and him. She saw I had his full attention as I climbed into the tub—*ahh!* Warm water—how long it had been! I unbraided my queue and dipped my head all the way under. I was in a thick, quiet world; it seeped into my saddle-weary muscles. I wanted Na-tio in the bath with me.

When I came up, Mary was still looking at Na-tio watching me. In a flash, she was out of her bloomers and in the tub, too. She was rewarded with Na-tio's friendly smile. He moved over to the window to beat dust from her dress. "This will be clean like you," he promised her.

Before Mary could change her mind, I grabbed the soap and scrubbed.

🌿 29 🌿

A DIFFERENT WAY

Na-tio wandered down the staircase to the shiny room below. Yipee's cleaning and combing was taking a while.

Why did Yipee want to give away Mary? Na-tio had pulled her from the ground. Mary liked him best of all. Yipee said that riding the cattle trail was no good, but Na-tio had always ridden and walked, ever since he was little.

This downstairs was empty except for one man, who was sitting at a far table. He turned when the last stair creaked under Na-tio's feet and pushed back his wide-brimmed hat as if to see Na-tio better.

He was no Anglo—this man was his people! Na-tio was sure of it—the same one he saw in Prescott, all that time ago. He looked so much like Mother's cousins, Na-tio had to catch his breath. But he kept his face still, his eyelids low.

"What a strange place for two such as us to meet." This man

in Anglo clothes, he used Anglo manners, too. He stood and gestured that Na-tio might wish to join him. Na-tio crossed the wide space around scattered tables and chairs to reach him. They stood together.

They discussed people, learning that, yes, they were related through cousins and clans. He came from those who traveled the eastern mountains. But he did not travel with them anymore.

"Let us walk," he suggested. "I am lonely to speak my language again." Na-tio agreed. He was lonely for his language, too.

The man introduced himself as Goylah. They walked around the back, through the yards behind. Goylah told Na-tio about his house—an Anglo house with land—and how he bred horses for cash money.

They passed an Anglo girl, sweating over a great iron pot. But she was not cooking. Na-tio saw fabric swirling there, like the fabric that covered the beds upstairs. She stirred and pounded it with a long stick.

Goylah wanted a wife, he said. A Pueblo woman, maybe. Someone who was accustomed to living in one place. Someone who grew plants—corn and squash. He talked of many things, this Goylah. He had strange ideas.

"Oh, wait," Goylah used Anglo-language to say his next words, "I have business here."

Na-tio was guided toward an open shed. He could see the town road on the other side. Inside the shed there was a big fire, like for the branders' irons at roundup. But the man at this fire was beating the white-hot metal with a hammer. Na-tio followed Goylah into the heat.

The other man was happy to see Goylah. He sunk the metal into water; steam rose and the water sizzled. Then those two talked, heads together. Na-tio had never seen such a friendly Anglo. But he didn't want to stare, so he looked at the things in the shop. It must be a shop, because no one needed so many copies of the same tools.

Then everything became strange, because Na-tio was shaking the Anglo's hand—Goylah was presenting him to the metal-worker. The metal-worker had bought a steer from the boss's herd. He was happy to have beef again.

Both men talked a great deal, but they wanted to listen, too, so Na-tio told them about finding Mary. They liked the story very much. Then there was more hand-shaking, and the metal-worker said Na-tio should "drop by any time." This seemed to mean that Na-tio should feel welcome to visit the metal-worker again. Well. Maybe Na-tio would.

On the way back to the hotel, Goylah explained how he and the metal-worker were breeding horses together.

They were partners? Na-tio stopped. He turned to stare. Goylah would partner with an Anglo? Next he would say he did business with soldiers!

Under Na-tio's hard eyes, Goylah's face dropped. "It is not the same, this life." He sighed, and the lines grew long around his mouth.

"But I choose this for my reasons."

Goylah seemed to grow taller as his gaze pierced Na-tio. He glanced at Na-tio's red shirt, the kerchief and trousers, before looking straight again. "I expect you have reasons, too."

For a moment, all the world was in those eyes. Na-tio didn't look away. He saw hurt and anger. He saw people lost like missing limbs. He felt his own heaviness in those eyes—his headaches, his unchangeable memories. Then those eyes shone with water and went blurry, because Na-tio's eyes were swimming, too.

They all had reasons. They all were finding a way.

"Of course," Na-tio agreed. "Of course."

Na-tio and Goylah walked in silence after that. Na-tio's head was crowded with too many different thoughts. And Goylah seemed to be thinking, too. When they parted, Na-tio promised he would visit Goylah's house-and-land, if ever he was passing. He wished that Goylah would find a good wife. Goylah wished that Na-tio would find what he was looking for.

Goylah was a strange kind of a man, but he was good.

RAQUEL RIVERA

➤ 30 ➤

THE BABY

By the time we were downstairs in the saloon, Mary's wet hair was already coming loose from the ribbon. I stopped to fix it—again. Na-tio was waiting for us at a far table.

"Why worry what this lady thinks?" he said. "Mary will stay with us. No problem."

I stood up, giving Mary's hair one last pat. "The trail is no place for a child." I had said this many times already. Na-tio never listened. "You will see I am right. Mrs. Willet is a good mother for Mary." Na-tio was wearing his stone-face, so I didn't wait for an answer.

"Mary?" I called. Where had she gone? That girl moved fast.

Mary was beside the long, shiny bar. "Look what I found!" She was near the little gate that kept the customers from going behind. There was a child on the other side, smaller than Mary. He was pulling himself to stand, using the slats of the gate. He was still too little to stand on his own.

"We must go." I moved to Mary, reaching for her hand. The baby let go and sat down hard. Then pulled himself back up. It was strange to see a baby in a saloon. "You have found a friend," I told Mary, wiggling my fingers so she would take my hand. We had to go.

The baby sat again. Why did he look familiar? Was it the red hair? Or was it the curls that made me think of someone? But I did not know any children besides Mary. I turned to Na-tio, who was standing like a statue over there. "Mrs. Willet would never keep a child in a saloon," I called.

"What can I get you?" The barkeep came out from the back, wiping his hands on his long apron. I shook my head, smiling to be friendly. He must think I was shouting for service.

"Why have you locked him up?" Mary's shrill voice echoed through the empty saloon.

The barkeep smoothed his mustaches, considering the question. "This here fellow? He is an unrepentant criminal doing hard time." He looked at me and winked. "Upstairs, he got into Big Ellen's face powder. She's got to clean up her room before the customers start asking for her." He took a rag from his apron pocket and put more shine on the bar.

"He was dropped off just this morning. We took him offa trapper who was bringing him from a farm that couldn't keep him no more, after they got him offa traveling pedlar. The girls upstairs said they'd watch him 'til the nuns come fetch 'im. They keep orphans, the nuns. Goats, too."

The barkeep raised his chin, calling to Na-tio, "You sure I can't get you something?" His mustaches waved with his breath.

Na-tio shook his head. He was tired of our chatter. But he didn't want to go to Mrs. Willet, either. He stood still.

"Suit yourself." The barkeep shrugged. "Everyone calls him Lucky," he said, nodding down at the baby.

"Hello, Lucky." Mary reached through the gate to pat his curls.

"He's mute." The barkeep told her. "Never makes a sound." He turned to me. "Maybe on account of being kidnapped by Indians—" Then his eyes went wide, seeing he was talking to me and Na-tio. "Well, that's what we were told," he declared, wiping the bar some more. He glared at Na-tio, daring him to say different.

Na-tio shifted from one leg to the other, crossing his arms. He said nothing, but the stone-face had left him. He probably wanted to hear more of Lucky's story, like me and Mary did.

"Well, maybe he was just born like that. Nobody knows," the barkeep admitted. "There was a hole in him, though—that's certain—went near through 'im, they say. Missed every important part. He's lucky, all right. Here ..." The barkeep bent down and pulled up Lucky's shirt. Lucky wriggled and squirmed, but the barkeep had a firm hand. "You can see the scar—perfect little circle—there's no denying it's from an arrow ..." he called over to Na-tio.

That's when I understood: I did know Lucky. The red hair. He was bigger now, of course. He was the baby from the cabin. I supppose I was the one who kidnapped him. That pedlar did what she promised; she kept him alive.

I leaned over the little gate and put my finger to the scar. Lucky twisted away, glaring at us all. The barkeep stood up, shrugging.

It was so long ago that I had stuffed that wound with an old quilt. Lucky had grown very much. But thinking back on that time, I felt as if I had grown more.

Na-tio finally moved to us, as if he was walking through a swamp–dragging himself.

"Are you all right?" His face had gone pale. Even in the dim saloon, I could see sweat glistening on his forehead. When Na-tio reached us, he actually fell on his knees. Mary rushed to him.

"Is that red hair?" he croaked. "That boy has red hair."

"Don't you like red hair?" Mary asked. "I think it's pretty."

"Let me see the scar," Na-tio demanded. This time, Lucky pulled his own shirt up. He was no longer wiggly, but he was glaring at us still. He stared at Na-tio. They both stared, like a hungry wolf sizing up a rattlesnake. Who was the wolf and who was the snake, I couldn't say. They both looked so fierce.

Then Na-tio reached, slowly, slowly, toward the scar. Lucky kept staring. Na-tio's eyes seemed to melt in his face. Were those tears? Maybe it was the bad light in here. When Na-tio touched the thick, puckered skin, Lucky smiled.

"Ow," he said.

Na-tio slumped to the ground next to Mary. He held onto the gate between him and Lucky as if it was keeping him from dropping flat.

The barkeep didn't even notice; he was too busy calling upstairs, "Hey! The kid speaks just fine ... who said he was mute?"

I had never seen Na-tio like this, not even in the cave with all the murdered ghosts. Now it was as if he had lost all his bones. The barkeep helped me bring Na-tio to a bar stool, then served him a whiskey. Na-tio pushed it aside and asked for water. His eyes were stuck on Lucky. Mary stroked his hand. I remembered when it was just Na-tio and me, when we camped near Mary's family. I remembered Na-tio's story by the fire.

Lucky had stopped pulling himself up on the gate. Now he kept pointing to his scar and laughing, "Ow!"

Na-tio shuddered every time. It was a fun game. For Lucky, anyway.

"Is this the baby you killed?" I whispered in his ear. I didn't want the barkeep or Mary to hear. Na-tio nodded, then shook his head. Then he nodded again.

"It cannot be," he said.

"I know this baby," I told him. "I found this baby. He had an arrow in him. Sharpened to a good point. No barb." Na-tio's eyes were growing bigger as I spoke. I stopped because I was afraid he might fall again.

"Go on," he growled.

"He was in a cabin." Na-tio was nodding at me. Those were tears, I was sure now. "The parents were ... there was blood everywhere." The whole story spilled out in a rush: about digging the grave, and the wound that was still alive. Na-tio's head dropped to the bar. Mary stood on her stool to stroke his hair.

"He's not feeling well," she explained to the barkeep and little Lucky. "Haven't you ever seen anyone being sad?"

"Go on!" Na-tio's voice was muffled behind his arms.

So I told him about the quilt, and the pedlar, and her bottle, and her breast. By now the barkeep was goggle-eyed. He pointed at me. "So *you're* the kidnapping Indians?" he scoffed.

Na-tio's shoulders started shaking and he finally lifted his head; he was laughing. Lucky laughed along with him. They had a long laugh together. Mary climbed on Na-tio's back she was so jealous.

Then Na-tio stood up, hitching her higher so she was comfortable to carry. I was glad to see his bones had returned.

"Good-bye, Lucky, we have to go now." He twisted his head to avoid Mary's hand as she tried to cover his mouth. "It was very nice to meet you! Very, very nice!"

On the way to Mr. and Mrs. Willet, Na-tio joked and smiled and laughed with me and Mary both. I had seen Na-tio smile before but now I understood: I had never seen him happy.

❧ 31 ❧

MR. AND MRS. WILLET

Mr. Willet was tall and thin like his wife. They could have been brother and sister. He put down his Bible and stood up from his desk when Mrs. Willet introduced the three of us: me, Na-tio, and Mary. He shook hands with a little bow, reserving his deepest bow for Mary. He was as good as Mrs. Willet. Everything was better than I even hoped.

Except Mary's new home was more bare than I imagined. There were no frilly curtains, no bookshelves. This sitting room was open with the kitchen. That closed door must be the bedroom. Maybe they were waiting for their things to arrive. Mrs. Willet had said they were new in town.

She tried to bring Mary into the kitchen, promising her fresh bread and butter, but Mary wouldn't go without Na-tio.

Mr. Willet asked me to sit, offering his chair.

"I have told Mrs. Willet we will take Mary," he said, as he

cleared a space among his papers and leaned against his desk. The only other seat in the room was a long settee in front of the fireplace. "You are, I understand, seeking a good home for her." I nodded and he continued. "Mrs. Willet explained the whole story. It is a wonder that you and your friend found her." He touched his Bible. "I don't speak of miracles lightly. It is not for sinners to judge which are God's miracles. But Mary's story is remarkable, indeed."

Mr. Willet pushed himself off the desk and invited me to join him on the porch. As we passed the kitchen, I saw Mary, both hands around a thick slice of bread. Na-tio was accepting a cup of tea with sugar, and Mary was quiet, even though they sat apart. Mrs. Willet looked up as we passed. Her pale face was flushed and her eyes glistened. She looked very happy.

"She feels truly blessed," Mr. Willet murmured as if to himself. "She has such a loving nature—enough for a dozen children."

The porch had a pretty view. From this side, the hills were green. The other side was ripped by the black, gaping mouths of the mines, with tracks and carts stretching out like tongues.

Stars were already winking in the sky. But Mr. Willet was staring at the graveyard. The crosses stuck out like pins on a pincushion— higgledy-piggledy, Jack would have called them. Some were just simple sticks tied with twine. Others were whitewashed boards nailed together. Only one cross had been turned and carved by carpenter's tools; the one with the flower garden.

Mr. Willet sighed at the graveyard. "Yes, enough for a dozen children—it was her dearest wish. And now she mustn't have any more the doctor says."

"You will both take good care of Mary," I assured Mr. Willet. They were thoughtful and kind people. They had a roof to give her. This was better than a cattle trail. Surely better also than Lucky's orphanage with the nuns and goats.

We went back inside. Mrs. Willet fluttered around us. Excitement made her tremble, rattling the cups and saucers. Without a coat and bonnet, she looked frail but bright—like a tall flower with a heavy blossom on top. She sat down to her own tea, beaming. How lucky Mary was. I took a sip. Mrs. Willet offered me the sugar. She had a little pitcher full of milk, too. Sugar and milk in tea?

Na-tio caught my shudder and smiled. He took a drink from his own sweet cup. Na-tio was fond of sugar.

"I am certainly pleased to make the acquaintance of Mr. Na-tio." Mrs. Willet nodded in his direction. Na-tio nodded back. "I told him I was forever grateful to him for finding Mary. You have both done such a fine job caring for her. I wonder how you managed!" She poured a drop of tea in Mary's cup, which was mostly milk. Mary pushed her empty plate aside to reach for it.

"What do we say, Mary?" Mrs. Willet asked, her voice as soft as flower petals. Mary paused, looking to Na-tio for the answer.

"We say 'thank you very much,' dear." Mrs. Willet held the cup back, waiting for Mary's response.

"T'ankyouverymuch," she said, both hands out for her cup. After she took a drink, Mary turned to Na-tio, "Can she tell me what to do?"

Mr. Willet looked stern but Mrs. Willet just laughed. "It's perfectly understandable." Her voice was like flower petals *and* rain. "Mary has been through many adventures. I'm sure her manners will return very soon." She stroked Mary's head. "'She' is the cat's mother, dear. You may call me—" Mrs. Willet suddenly looked worried. "What shall Mary call us, Mr. Willet, until she learns to feel at home?"

"This is a very nice house." Na-tio startled us all by speaking. "Yipee told me that you are good, and now I see this myself." He put both hands on the table and nodded, first at Mrs. Willet and then at Mr. Willet. "You will make fine parents. Any child will be lucky to have you."

We all smiled at the polite words, then waited. It was clear he had more to say. This was surprising; Na-tio rarely had much to say. "Yipee wants this for Mary, and I think I understand why. But I must explain to you both that Mary stays with me."

Mary looked up from her teacup. "What? Of course I am with you—you found me!"

The pretty color left Mrs. Willet's cheek. She forgot to correct

Mary, who should have said, "I beg your pardon," not "What." Even I know that.

"Come now." Mr. Willet's eyebrows rose high during Na-tio's speech, and now they were meeting above his nose. "You're not suggesting that you take on the care of this child, sir? You're not fit to raise a little girl; *you* are—" Whatever Mr. Willet was going to say did not come out. He had slammed his mouth down on it. When his lips opened again, they breathed, "The idea is preposterous."

"Na-tio?" Mary put down her teacup and, before I could blink, she had slipped off her chair and was beside him. Mary moved fast.

Mrs. Willet turned on me, her eyes like a hunted animal. "You said we should have her—you know it's for the best!"

Mary's arms were clasped around Na-tio. "No!" she sobbed. Then she started to scream.

Mary's voice was very loud. I covered my ears. I should have known she would not be left easily. Couldn't she see this was the proper place for her? Na-tio and I had other things to do. I would explain to Na-tio that he was denying Mary her best chance.

"Let me talk to them!" My voice echoed inside my covered ears. I used my elbow to point to the porch. Na-tio stood, taking Mary's hand. She went quiet and put her thumb in her mouth.

When we were outside, I kneeled down to wipe her face. "You are a mess," I scolded her. "What will they think?" I looked to the kitchen window. It was filled with the shadows of Mr. and Mrs. Willet. The shadows jumped and moved away.

Mary stood still, letting me wipe her nose. "I don't want to live with them." She didn't try to shout, but Mary had what Jack would call a "carrying voice." What if the Willets could hear?

"Shh. You are just a little girl. You do not decide. Now, be good."

I stood up, wishing I was not quite so small and Na-tio was not so tall. "You agreed!" I reminded him. I tried to put much feeling in my whisper. I was also trying to remember if Na-tio had actually agreed to my plan. "You said yourself they are good. And they are her people."

"Excuse me," Mary said in a quiet voice for a change. "They are not."

She sniffled and took the handkerchief I held out. "My people were going to come back for me, but they can't now because they died—Mama, Daddy, and my brothers. All I have is Na-tio, who found me."

She was as stubborn as Crooked Mah, this one!

Oh. Wait.

I had forgotten that Crooked Mah had raised me. He had found me, too. Suddenly, I felt empty with missing him too much. Crooked Mah would know what to do. He always had an answer.

I didn't want to be confused. I just wanted to be back on the cattle trail with Na-tio.

Na-tio's warm hands rested on my shoulders, then slid down my arms. I leaned into him. "Don't worry for this," his breath tickled the top of my head. "These Willets are good enough. They will make a good family. Let me talk to Mary. You go inside."

If there was anyone more determined than Mary, it must be Na-tio because, only moments later, they were back in the kitchen. Mary was as good as gold, going with Mrs Willet to the wash basin, for bedtime. "This has been a big day for all of us, hasn't it, Mary?" Mrs Willet said.

Mr Willet was shaking Na-tio's hand up and down so hard, I thought they might lift off the ground. He was glad to see that Na-tio was a man of reason after all, he said. He had no doubt of Na-tio's warm feelings for the child, he said. Who wouldn't, after what they had been through together? But Mary needed a roof over her head and an education befitting her kind.

His hand going up and down, Na-tio wore a little smile.

Na-tio took me back to the room that night. He wanted a roof for me, too, he said. The cattle trail was good enough for me, but I didn't argue because I wanted us to be alone. Soon we would be back at work, with all the hands and hundreds of steer. When would we get another chance to be together under blankets?

We hugged and kissed all over. Na-tio stroked my hair, making shivers down my back. He lay his long body over me and

RAQUEL RIVERA

I held on for dear life. I'd never let go, I told him, shuddering like a mountain crumbling under nitro—like he was shuddering, too. And sounds came to us—from us—like I had never heard before. We were animals; we were one animal.

As I drifted off on the crook of his arm, my spit made a puddle on his chest. I closed my mouth and hoped he didn't mind, because I couldn't move from this warm, wet, perfect place. Maybe he was asleep already. Me, I couldn't move; not for anything.

Then he was shaking me awake. "It's time," he was whispering in my ear. "We have to go."

But it was still dark. I tried to roll over but he took the blankets. He made me put on my clothes and my boots. Mumbling and yawning, I let him lead me down the wide stairs, through the empty saloon. Here, night was over—just a few tipped chairs and empty glasses from the last customers and hotel guests, now gone to bed.

But it still wasn't morning, either. Outside, it was dark and cold. I buttoned my coat as Na-tio unhitched the horses. Wait—where did he get those horses? And why were our things tied on? Why did he have our bundles and our sleeping rolls?

"Now we get Mary." Na-tio whispered as he gave me a lift onto the saddle.

I must have misheard him. I was still half-asleep as we rode through town, to the little clapboard house with the pretty view. Wait, what had Na-tio said?

When we dismounted, I saw he was carrying another bundle under his coat. The bundle seemed to move. Maybe I was stlll dreaming. No, there it was again; the bundle was moving!

I grabbed Na-tio. "What are you doing?" I hissed. He turned and smiled, showing me Lucky's chubby face, fast asleep in his arms.

"What is this?" I squeaked. But he was gone before I could even blink.

He slipped across the porch like a shadow, just like when he saved me and Blackie from the wolf, before we even knew each other. I crept to the front window and saw him bending over the settee, putting down Lucky and picking up Mary.

Lucky deserved a nice home—but leave Mary, too!

Mrs. Willet would be happy to have another child; Mr. Willet had said she wanted a dozen. Why, she could start an orphanage like the nuns. Or just keep Mary and Lucky, like daughter and son.

There was no changing Na-tio's mind. He was just like when he took the horses from the skin-collector.

I must explain better. I would say all the good reasons we could not raise Mary. I would remember what Jack and the boss had said about it. For now, I helped him tie on Mary. If I explained well, surely he would turn around and give her back.

As the horses carried us toward the hills, I thought I saw the bedroom light go on. Maybe Lucky had woken up. The Willets would be very surprised; they weren't used to Na-tio the way I was.

RAQUEL RIVERA

❧ 32 ❧

THE LAND

Yipee was mad and Na-tio knew why. By keeping Mary, it meant they could not travel with the herd. Yipee thought someone else should look after Mary, not her and Na-tio.

"Mary can live in a comfortable house," Yipee had told him, as the shadows of the town disappeared behind hills.

Na-tio didn't think house-living was as comfortable as camping. Mary's warm, sleeping body was heavy on his back as they bumped along. She was comfortable. Na-tio was comfortable, too.

"A child needs a mother." Yipee said. She sounded like that Jack.

"Or a Crooked Mah," Na-tio reminded her. Under the moonlight, Na-tio saw she smiled at that one. She was quiet for a while.

Then, "Why?" Yipee threw up her hands, forgetting about her reins; the horse's head jerked back. "Just say why! What is so special about Mary?"

That was a difficult one.

Pulling Mary out of the ground, it was the opposite of killing a baby, maybe. It was Na-tio's chance to do better. That was something.

Then, it was Mary. She was strong and lively, even though she had no family anymore. Na-tio admired and respected this.

"She is like me. Like you," he told Yipee.

"There are orphans everywhere we go," Yipee muttered. "Many orphans."

Maybe. But they weren't as good as Mary. Mary made Na-tio's mind too busy to feel sad and heavy. With Mary, Na-tio saw a way for himself. He could show her traveling and camping. As sure as mountains and sky were true, these were good things Mary could learn.

Even after a long sleep, Yipee was unhappy. "They treated us fair at Double Y, and now we have taken their horses ..." Na-tio knew she was thinking of their own horses, the ones they took from the skin-collector. The Paint and the others were now waiting for them to return to the ranch. But Yipee said nothing, hanging her kettle over the fire. She was making porridge for Mary, for them all.

They had stopped by a creek, under a stand of trees that gave shade. Na-tio had already found a branch that he could make into a small bow for Mary. It was good they were back on the land. Yipee was right: the cattle-trail was no place for a child. It was no place for any person.

RAQUEL RIVERA

He cut along the branch with his knife to make it smooth and the same size all around. Then there would be soaking and pulling, and tying the ends so it curved well, before hardening it in fire.

Mary wanted to try cutting a branch, too. Na-tio promised she could, soon. He didn't smile because this was serious, and Mary must watch to learn.

Yipee was quiet, but her anger bristled high, like her top-hair.

"We had a place—I had a place—on this crazy Gold Mountain," she finally said. She told Na-tio it was a bad idea to leave the herd, the boss, and the others. "They treat us well; we are given pay. We are useful at the ranch. Why do you not like this?"

He just didn't like it. Na-tio's way was different. Or it would be different as soon as he found it. Why didn't Yipee understand *this?*

"It was exactly as I wanted," Yipee complained, stirring the pot. "We were useful among people, living well and being safe. This is how we survive this rough, killing place."

"I can be your people," Na-tio told her, but she didn't seem to hear. "Mary can be your people."

Now they were tying up a blanket to shield Mary from the sun. Na-tio gave her the bow-branch to hold, while she took a nap.

Yipee whispered, "It is too difficult to care for a child." She brushed a fly from Mary's sleeping face. "I don't want this," she grumbled.

Na-tio didn't want this, either. He didn't want Mother gone

and Father fighting Anglos far away. He knew Yipee thought this camping, this traveling, was not a real place. But she didn't know the land like Na-tio. She didn't know it was the most important place. "My people are useful," he told her.

He wouldn't say the rest out loud. His people lived well, too— long before this ugly, busy world of soldiers and settlers. Na-tio would not pass any more seasons driving the Anglos' meat-slaves across the land. He wanted to find his own way.

But he didn't say this because Yipee would get more angry. He wished that Yipee would be happy.

When Mary woke, the porridge was ready. She climbed on his back as he squatted by the fire. "Eat," Na-tio urged her and Yipee. They all dipped into the pot.

"*Nyum, nyum, nyum,*" Mary made a little sound when she ate. "I like the seeds," she hummed. Yipee had remembered this plant from the last time they camped, and had shaken the seeds into the oats. Na-tio would gather more. It was good if Mary liked food from the land.

"Oh!" Mary dropped her spoon. It clattered into the pot. Her little face went long, her mouth open and round. "You forgot to say thank-you-Lord!" She was staring at them both, Yipee and Na-tio. "Mama says thank-you-Lord before we eat." Then her face softened on them, like they were the children. "I had to teach Cook, too."

Yipee slapped at a mosquito. "Any time is all right to say thank you," she suggested, shrugging at Na-tio.

"This is true." Na-tio agreed.

Mary's eyebrows came together as she picked up her spoon. She raised it to her lips, her brows rising with it. She paused, pale eyes darting, and breathed, "Thank-you-Lord," before popping in the mouthful.

Na-tio could feel Yipee's eyes on him but he wouldn't look her way. They would both laugh, and that wasn't right to Mary. They must get used to one another's ways. Then everyone was quiet, in their own thoughts, until the pot was empty.

Yipee leaned back. "We must return these horses to Double Y," she said, sucking her teeth. "Our horses wait for us, too."

Since they had left their horses at the ranch, Na-tio thought they might keep these ones. This would be trade, not raiding, so Yipee shouldn't be bothered.

But he wished that Yipee be happy, so he agreed.

CHAPTER

 33

BACK AT THE RANCH

"Blackie!" My horse ran to the fence when I called. She looked fatter. She was enjoying her holidays too much. Na-tio clicked his tongue and the others came, too. He offered handfuls of dark berries we had gathered that morning.

"Starfire wants some, too," I laughed, as the owner's fine red horse nudged his way between the Paint and Na-tio's favorite. That's when I saw Mr. Holt coming from the stables. They must have told him we were here. I took my hand from Starfire's soft nose.

"Starfire's happy to see you boys again." Mr. Holt shoved up his hat brim. "'Cept now I'm short hands on the trail. What in hell you doing back here?" He spat a stream of tobacco at the fence post.

Mary was crouched behind the same post, poking a beetle with a stick. Now she stood up, shouting, "I know what that is—my daddy likes a chaw!" Mr. Holt jumped like she was a rattlesnake. I tried not to smile.

RAQUEL RIVERA

While she climbed up Na-tio's leg, I explained to Mr. Holt about finding her, and how she couldn't ride the cattle trail all day long. I told him how we gave her to the Willets, but they took a little boy instead. Of course, I didn't explain how that had all happened.

"So you brought her here." Mr. Holt seemed to think this was a bad idea.

"Well, yes," I admitted, at the same time that Na-tio said, "No."

What? I turned to him.

"We bring you the trail horses we borrowed," Na-tio explained. "Mary stays with me." His dark eyes were drilling into mine. His mouth was set in its thin line. It was like he had decided something at that moment. Or maybe he had decided before. Maybe I just hadn't seen it.

I felt a tickle in my throat and my mouth twitched. Na-tio would not stay and work the ranch as I wanted to do.

He had tried, like I had asked, so I couldn't say he didn't know. He did know. I could stop pretending he might change.

There was a funny feeling in my stomach, like the bottom had dropped. It was a stretching, empty feeling. I had finally lost. Or maybe I had always lost. I tried to keep my mouth straight and firm like Na-tio. But I didn't want him to leave—more than ever.

When he wanted to fight the soldiers who killed his family, I shouted to make him stay. When he wouldn't try ranch work,

I changed his mind with a red flannel shirt. Every time he stayed, it was only harder to think of letting go. Now was the hardest of all; now I knew his face, his body—his moods—better than my own.

But there was no more trying in me. There was no use to keep trying; that's what his eyes were telling me.

"Excuse, please," I managed to say, before I ran.

My sight was so blurry and I ran so hard, I didn't stop until I hit a tree.

I sat, rubbing my bruised shoulder. I could see them from here; they looked small. Na-tio held Mary as she sat on the fence. Mr. Holt was showing her how to stroke Starfire's nose. It looked like Na-tio was talking to Mr. Holt. It seemed like Na-tio talked to everyone now. He used to leave the talking to me.

Not anymore, I thought, which made me cry again. As I threw myself down, the grass tickled my ears. Rolling over, I stared up through the fan-shaped leaves. I squeezed my eyes until the blue sky pushed forward, turning the green and gold leaves into background.

I saw pictures of Na-tio. When we first met and I bandaged his wound. When he gave me the Paint in that bright, warm meadow. When his straight mouth went soft for me under blankets.

There was no use thinking. I pressed my hands into my eyes to squash the pictures. After all, I would not join Na-tio, either: always camping, never arriving. Crooked Mah and I traveled, too, but we didn't want to. We wanted to stay and build, to find our fortune. Crooked Mah made me learn English so I could find my way. I closed my eyes and felt the leaf-shadows move across my face.

Then Na-tio found Mary. That must have made him decide. I wished to hate her but it wasn't her fault. Mary was Na-tio's fortune. Then he met Lucky, too, so naturally he feels much better now. I should be happy for him. I *am* happy for him. I'm sad for me.

"Why are you crying, Yipee? Daddy says crying is for babies." Mary was squatting by my ear, not shouting for once, patting my head like I was Blackie. I wiped my eyes. Her chubby legs were all scratched from yesterday, when she was reaching for the delicious red fruit on a cactus. "I'm being careful," she had replied after I warned her, but she had forgotten the spiny paddles near the ground.

I touched the wounds. "You told me your daddy died while you were in the ground." I said. This was a question I had wondered about for a while. "Why do you talk as if he and your mama are still with us?"

Mary looked confused. "They are." It was obvious, her expression said. When she saw I didn't understand, she explained. "They said they would never leave me. When they put me in the box, they said they would never leave me."

I looked back up through the leaves. I wondered if maybe

Crooked Mah was also with us. It did seem at times I could hear his voice—even if it was coming out my own throat. Maybe Mary should tell Na-tio this. Maybe Na-tio's mother was here, too. I was beginning to see why Na-tio insisted on keeping Mary. Strange to think, but I would miss her, too.

Na-tio squatted down by my other ear. "That owner likes you with Starfire. You are weak for calf-wrestling but good with horses," he murmured. "You can stay."

I felt silly, stretched out like a dead body. I sat up, blowing my nose into my sleeve. Mary offered me a drink from the canteen—the first practical thing I knew her to do. I drank.

"But we don't want you to stay, Yipee. We want you with us." Mary had the blinking-est eyes I ever saw.

I started re-braiding her hair to make it tidy. She insisted on wearing it in a single queue like mine. "You take the Paint," I told her and turned to Na-tio. "She better have the Paint. You take them all—I'll just keep Blackie." Every time I opened my mouth, it twisted with sadness. I gave Mary a squeeze to hide my tears. I mumbled into her sweaty neck, "Promise you will visit me."

Mary promised, but I didn't let go until Na-tio nodded, too.

A shadow cast over us. I jumped up, wiping my eyes and brushing at my clothing. It was Mr. Holt.

"I hope you ain't crying over my invitation to stay." His mouth turned around his tobaccco so much, it was difficult to know if he was angry or smiling. I nodded, shook my head, then nodded again.

"This is my dream. To be with the horses." I sniffed hard. If he said I was too weak because of crying, I would say there was grass in my eye.

"I reckon it's a dream that suits you, Yipee. As it happens, I could use a stable hand with a sweet touch." Then he shook my hand like we were in business together. I was smiling so wide, my face hurt by the time he took his leave.

He walked a few steps, then turned like he'd forgotten something.

"Oh, and Yipee, you'll bed down in the tack room from now on. Tell the housekeeper to set you a cot." He spat a tobacco stream toward the paddock.

"The bunkhouse is no fit place for a girl." Mr. Holt continued on his way.

My smile dropped. Everything went misty for a moment. I could feel Na-tio beside me, shaking with laughter.

"Did you tell?" I hissed.

"I never tell." He raised his hands like he was surrendering. "I think you make a very good boy," he said, his eyes still laughing.

I huffed, turning away from him. "Yes, sir!" I called before Mr. Holt walked out of hearing. Before he could change his mind. "I'll surely do that!"

All this time, I had left places when I would rather have stayed, like the railway camp and Mrs. Hall's little ranch. Now I was finally staying.

Now I was the one left behind.

I helped tie Mary to Na-tio's back one last time. He would travel far today. The Paint was tied to his saddle. Na-tio wanted both horses to get used to this so Mary could ride soon. Mr. Holt had the housekeeper pack them provisions. This kindness made me glad. It showed I was staying in the right place.

"Yipee," Na-tio said. He squeezed my hand. "Yipee."

I looked up. He was blocking the sun, his face in shadow. He put his warm hand around my cheek. "So round." He said it soft and low, like when it was just the two of us. "I always like to see your round face, since the very first time."

"Don't forget about our calf. We still share the calf," I reminded him. "He has our brand." I squeezed my eyes shut and wished hard.

You will come back to me; you *will* come back.

I think some of it leaked out loud, because Na-tio smiled at me.

"You and me," he said. "I like that; you and me."

He seemed so sure. But I had many questions whirling inside. When would they visit? How would I know they were coming? Would he send word if he needed help? How would they ever find me if I had to leave the ranch?

He kept smiling and mounted his tall horse, Mary's legs kicking against him, and he looked so strong and beautiful that I didn't ask anything.

He was always my Na-tio, wherever the path took him and Mary.

I slapped the horse on the rump and they were on their way.

"You are a bright spot on the land, Yipee," he called back over Mary's waving arm. "It is always easy to find you."

ACKNOWLEDGMENTS

My thanks go to Shelley Tanaka for feedback on early drafts of the story, and to Peter Carver for helpful direction with its plot—long before he recommended (and ultimately edited) *Yipee* for Red Deer Press.

I am grateful to the Canada Council for the Arts for support in the creation of this book, which included funds for a research trip to Arizona. The Sharlot Hall Museum and Archives in Prescott was a treasure trove of information, as was the Desert Caballeros Museum in Wickenburg. The Museum of Northern Arizona in Flagstaff is a bounty for anyone interested in the cultures and pre-history of Indigenous peoples of the American Southwest.

I'm also grateful for conversation with Elizabeth, Apache-language teacher at the Yavapai-Apache Cultural Resource Center, in Camp Verde, AZ, and Apache Culture Manager Mr. Vincent Randall, and his uncle, who also shared knowledge with me. In our conversations, they showed me a very small glimpse of another side of the story. Perhaps one day we may all learn it–I hope so. In the meantime, this particular story of Yipee and Na-tio was significantly re-shaped by the brief time they spent with me and the knowledge they felt able to share.

My thanks also go to Yellowsnake, outfitter and guide, for his horseback tour through the hills of the Sonoran desert, for sharing his knowledge of pre-history and of the land, and for sharing his own story. (Yellowsnake's eventful life is also the subject of a very interesting book, *Yellowsnake: Son of Prophecy* by Jake Conrad.)

Finally, I'm very grateful to Dr. Sharon Moses of the Northern Arizona University, for reading *Yipee*, with particular attention to Apache cultural references in the story.

May *Yipee's Gold Mountain* be a credit to everyone's efforts. Any errors are mine.

Many books, periodicals, old photos, and even movies, helped bring substance and detail to the story of *Yipee's Gold Mountain*. Most helpful were: *Chinese in America* by Iris Chang (Viking, 2003); *Chinese American Voices: The Gold Rush to the Present*, edited by Judy Yung, Gordon H. Chang, Him Mark Lai (University of California Press, 2006); *Chinese Sojourners in Territorial Arizona* by Florence Lister and Robert Lister (Sharlot Hall Museum Press); *Indeh: An Apache Odyssey* by Eve Ball (Brigham Young University Press, 1980); *Apache: a History and Culture*

RAQUEL RIVERA

Portrait by James L. Haley (Doubleday, 1981); *Western Apache Raiding and Warfare*, edited by Keith H. Brasso (University of Arizona Press, 1971); *Apache Mothers and Daughters* by Ruth McDonald Boyer (University of Oklahoma Press, 1992). *Cowgirls: 100 years of Writing the Range*, edited by Thelma Poirier (Lone Pine, 1997); *The Complete Cowboy Reader: Remembering the Open Range*, edited by Ted Stone (Lone Pine, 1997); *Mustang: The Saga of the Wild Horse in the American West* by Deanne Stillman (Houghton Mifflin, 2008). The complete text of Mark Twain's reportage, read by Yipee to her teacher, can be found in *Mark Twain's Travels with Mr. Brown* (Russell & Russell, 1971).

Raquel Rivera

INTERVIEW WITH RAQUEL RIVERA

Why did you decide to focus on the experiences of a Chinese cowboy who was actually a girl?

I enjoy reading and writing about girls who succeed in breaking out of the restrictive social mores imposed on them. (There are heaps of these girls and women through history and today.) In mid-19th-century America, the "lawless" frontier offered a fighting chance to anyone who sought to live according to their own rules. For example, even though power and public life were uncommon for women, Elizabeth Smith, a black American, was an important founder of the town of Wickenburg, AZ. She ran the town's hotel and restaurant, was a respected investor in other local businesses and mines, and served in the municipal government.

Sharlot Hall was another woman who was able to lead an independent life in frontier society. By the early 1900s, she was appointed the New Territory of Arizona's official historian, thanks to her interest in preserving knowledge and artifacts of Arizona's history.

In frontier days, there were women working as cowboys, too, signing up to join their fellows on the trail, bringing cattle to market towns. Disguised as men for the duration of the job, they were often experienced ranchers who needed cash for their own establishments. One story tells of a properly dressed lady re-introducing herself to a surprised trail boss: "Why, don't you remember me?"

But as an imagined person, Yipee is unusual, in that I didn't find any examples of Chinese cowboys, men or women. In the Wild West, it seems that Chinese men worked as cooks, ran laundries, managed restaurants, mined claims, built railroads, and did agricultural work. At this time, there were few Chinese women in America, and their roles seem to have been limited to that of prostitute and the very occasional sequestered middle-class wife of a successful immigrant. I suppose in Yipee, I was writing a girl who I wish had been!

The story is set in Arizona in the 1860s. What will 21st-century young readers find in this period that is relevant to their lives?
I hope readers will see themselves in the story, and that this fraught moment in history can be a lesson for better cooperation today (as Yipee and Na-tio manage to do). I hope the story encourages the idea that even during conflict, it's necessary to keep an open mind and heart.

There is a good deal of violence in this story: the Apaches under Na-tio's father kill a settler and his wife; soldiers slaughter all the people in Na-tio's extended family—and there's more. Why was it important that these scenes be included in the story?

The violent scenes are reflective of the times, which were driven by episodes of attack, retribution, and further revenge for retributions past. Na-tio's part of the story shows the lasting damage this approach inflicts on individuals and nations. The violent scenes also provide a contrast to Na-tio's growing strength and imagination as he attempts to transform the vicious circle.

What are the challenges for an author who wants to write about a time and place that is not part of her own personal experience?

You know, I think that's the job of fiction writers: to artfully empathize, to explore unknown worlds—not to preach what we think we already know. In other words, I do tons of research and lots of thinking!

One of the themes that comes up over and over again is the false assumptions many of your characters make about each other. Why did you want to explore that idea?

I believe we all imagine fictions about one another, based on our own cultural backgrounds, personal experience, and dispositions. This can be positive when it creates goodwill and a sense of community. I was trying to show how misguided and unproductive it can be—especially in tense relationships.

Why would an Apache youth like Na-tio want to look after an "Anglo" child.

Researching and telling Na-tio's part of the story was often sad and difficult. Reading about the events of the so-called Apache Wars, over and over, in the different words of historians, made me feel regret. Regret for the greed of Anglo-Americans—and for the brutal violence from all. Most upsetting was how the few well-intentioned voices among the U.S. Army staff, government adminstrators, and local settlers seemed to be so easily drowned out by ignorant and malicious ones. By passing his knowledge to a younger "Anglo," Na-tio is doing what many Indigenous peoples did when they married and parented outside their cultures. This part was also written to symbolize an act of peace: Na-tio generously shares knowledge the "Anglo" culture so sorely needs, with someone who is ready to listen. Finally, it's a mature act, showing Na-tio's character arc from boy to young man. Personally, I think Na-tio is repairing wounds from his relationship with his own father by being a father to someone else. By caring for one another, we may find purpose and love.

Thank you, Raquel.